CHANGE OF COURSE

Joseph T. Klempner

To my brother. Who else?

FORWARD

I should explain that, by trade, I am a lawyer first and a writer only second, at least in terms of the path my life has taken. I've been a criminal defense attorney for thirty years, but it's only in the last few of those that I've found the time and inspiration to sit down and write half a dozen books. And as if that weren't reward enough in itself, I've now had the exceedingly good fortune to actually see a few of them published. As might be expected, they include a couple of legal thrillers" (as they like to call them in the trade), a "caper" (for lack of a better term), and several accounts of real cases I've handled over the years.

Taking stock recently of these accomplishments (modest enough by any objective standard, but nothing less than monumental to my way of thinking), it occurred to me that the only important book, about the singular event in my life that is truly worth telling, was the one conspicuous by its absence: the one I *hadn't* written.

This came as no startling revelation, understand. I'd known for some time that even by the process of turning out these "lawyer books" of mine, I'd been putting off recounting the one chapter of my life that totally dwarfs everything else I'd experienced in the forty-three years I'd lived before the event and the fifteen years since.

But on this particular occasion, my awareness was heightened, something caused me to react differently. To be sure, the process took a full month to play itself out - a month of denial, of procrastination, of deliberately busying myself with a slew of unimportant chores designed purely to distract me, to keep me a safe distance from what was so clearly calling me. It was a month of false starts and last-minute hesitations. Several times, I got as far as the door to the bottom of the old wooden stairs behind the kitchen, each time I got no farther. But I knew with each trip that I was getting closer, I was getting ready.

When I at last found myself opening the door and actually climbing the stairs, it seemed no great effort at all. It was as though the moment had finally arrived It was simply time.

I hadn't set foot in the attic for a decade and a half, and I saw right away that no one else had, either. I was struck not so much by the silence of the place as by its *stillness*. Nothing moved. No breeze reached here, no puff of air signaling the opening or closing of a door or window.

There was a pretty impressive mountain of clutter on top of the trunk: diving gear and sail bags, boxes of charts and manuals, nylon lines smartly coiled, winch handles that had once gleamed like silver in the sunlight. I set it all aside, my fingers leaving fresh prints in the dust that had been quietly at work entombing it all.

The trunk opened easily enough, ready at last to yield its cargo, as though it, too, sensed that the time had finally come.

A sextant and two compasses rested on top, a pair of dividers and a set of parallel rules, books of tide tables and stacks of weather reports. There were star charts, correction tables, and repair guides; there were binoculars and tools. There were flares that would no longer flare and an air horn that had leaked the last of its air, as well as a folded radar reflector and a rusted fog bell. There were all manner of flotation devices and foul-weather gear, moldy from dampness and the passage of time.

And at the bottom, right where I'd seen it in my mind's eye every day of these last fifteen years, there it was.

I took it in my hands and lowered myself to the floor, my back against the trunk. For a while, I did nothing but sit there, waiting for the trembling in my hands to subside. Then, carefully, I began stripping away the tissue paper from around it. Its red cover, faded and watermarked even before it had found its resting place, still bore the title that had been embossed in gold leaf, making it the handsome gift that it had been, presented to my brother by some friend whose name I can no longer remember.

The Log of the Sea Legs is all it said.

I opened it to what had been intended as a dedication page but had instead been used as a place for well-wishers to scribble their thoughts, a sort of "bon voyage" autograph page, not unlike what one might expect to find in a high school yearbook. As the names rushed back to me from over the years, a faded Polaroid photograph slipped from the book. In the half-light of the attic, I had difficulty making out the faces, but I knew most of them just the same. Looking back at me were my wife and our three children, my brother Jack's ex-wife and their two children, and a good dozen friends, relatives, and well-wishers who'd joined us at the dock. There'd been broad smiles and crisp laughter in the warm sunshine that saw the two of us off that day. Someone holds an oversized bottle of champagne aloft, and the camera catches the sun glinting off it. We are all standing in front of *Sea Legs,* the single-masted sloop that was to be home for Jack and me for the next three months as we headed out into the open waters of the Atlantic. In the photo, she is freshly painted and scrubbed, her brass shined, and her teak oiled for whatever might lie ahead.

I turned the page and came upon the first entry in the log. The entries were all in my hand; Jack had refused to contribute. "You're the writer, Joe," he'd said at the time, though all I'd written by then was a single manuscript, which I'd stuffed into a closet along with a handful of rejection letters. But by default, I'd been put in charge of the log, and I'd accepted my assignment without objection. For the next three months, I'd chronicled our adventure by making entries into the book with the red cover and the gold lettering.

I'd tried to write something each day, and now - as I began turning the pages and reliving the voyage - I saw that I'd succeeded, for the most part. I was prolific some days and stingy others. There were even a few days with no entries at all. But the story was there; the story that I've been both putting off and getting ready to tell these last fifteen years.

There, too, folded in quarters and stuffed into the very back of the book, were a dozen or so sketches that Jack had done on board. Some of them were good, others no more than a line or two, suggesting the shape of a wave or the bend of a sail. I'd forgotten all about them.

My original thought was simply to edit and reproduce the original log entries, and I actually began doing just that. But very soon, I realized that to do so would be to ignore the fact that these last fifteen years have had their own impact on what happened; they have shaped the way I *feel* about the events. To deny the years the role they played in the process would, therefore, be to deny everything I'd been through since; the rage, the self-hatred, the struggle to understand, the long battle to forgive, accept, and go on. I decided that all of that aftermath had become part of the story, too, or at least how I'd come to see it. So I needed to tell it from here and from now.

This, then, is the story of our trip, the voyage of *Sea Legs* It is not a sailing primer, and the serious sailor will be disappointed if he's come aboard for a technical account of our months at sea. I have left it for other, more knowledgeable mariners to write about sailing dynamics, navigational techniques, and compass corrections. The difference between magnetic north and true north may be important business to those who go to sea under sail, but it can be pretty tedious stuff to the landlocked reader. My only resources have been the log itself and my own memory, sometimes imperfect, but sometimes so incredibly vivid that I find exact words and precise gestures are burned into my mind as though I'd lived them yesterday. I have edited some of the conversations between Jack and me, in an effort to provide better continuity and readability. But as to the content of those conversations, and as to the actual events that transpired, I have made no changes whatsoever: What follows is a faithful account of just what it was that happened back then aboard *Sea Legs* - to Jack and, ultimately, to me.

New York, New York
August 1996

1

It was sometime during the summer of the thirty-eighth year of his life that Jack found out he was sick. It had begun simply enough, with a routine visit to his doctor for a checkup. Or so we'd been told at the time. Later on, he admitted that he'd felt a lump here, or noticed a slight discoloration there, or had maybe lost a few pounds he couldn't quite account for.

He'd undergone some tests, and then some further tests to confirm what the first tests had showed. Jack hated everything about the testing process - the bother, the indignity, the considerable expense, and, above all, the deliberate reluctance of the medical professionals to look him square in the eye and tell him what he already had to have known: that this was a disease that was going to kill him - perhaps not imminently, nor even in a year or two, but soon enough.

There had followed a period of time during which Jack made

it his business to share the news with the people in his life who were closest to him. Those people included his former wife, whom he'd married before his twenty-first birthday and divorced just after his thirty-fifth, but with whom he still kept in touch and whom he saw from time to time. He liked to say that they'd finally become friends, and it truly seemed so. It included his twin daughters, who by that time were in their first year at a small private college in New England. It included a handful of aunts and uncles and cousins, but no parents - they'd died in their sixties, seven months apart to the day. And it included me, his older brother.

Comparing notes later on, it seems we all reacted to the news in pretty much the same way; disbelief, then denial, followed by anger at the unfairness of it, and then disbelief all over again at Jack's own apparent *lack* of anger, his willingness to accept the verdict without railing against whatever gods or odds had handed it down.

Jack had some work to finish up, and he set about attending to it. He hated leaving matters unfinished, whether that involved a project at the office, a chore in the backyard, or a meal on the table. He was absolutely driven in any endeavor he undertook (far more than I, who have always been happy to leave something for tomorrow), and he was good at almost everything he did. He was earning a decent living at the time, and even with two daughters to put through school, he had a comfortable place to live, an old Jeep to get him around, and some money in the bank. And, of course, he had his boat. And it was to his boat that Jack now turned his attention.

She was a thirty-six-foot fiberglass sloop he had bought at auction some eight or ten years earlier, at a time when buying a boat didn't necessarily require a mortgage, the way it does today. She'd been built in Sweden as an offshore racer but had spent her youth in and out of yacht clubs and marinas along the East Coast, in what might be likened to a series of one-night stands for a young lady with hopes of something more enduring. Jack had shown her a taste of that, taking her farther out than her previous owners, but the truth was that, for all our skills (and they were not inconsiderable), neither Jack nor I had ever done any long-distance sailing of the type that puts both man and boat to the test.

Now Jack pulled her out of the water in early autumn and had her put through all sorts of stress tests to determine if her hull was sound and her fittings tight. It occurred to me at the time that he was subjecting her to much the same scrutiny as he himself had recently undergone. But where the news on Jack had been bad, the report on his boat came back quite the opposite: She was pronounced structurally fit, in need only of some relatively minor modifications.

He spent all of that fall and much of that winter working on her. He reinforced the hull; he caulked and recaulked seams; he fitted steel plates to the interior and ballast to the keel; he added hundreds of pounds of fiberglass all around. He rerigged the lines so that they could be worked with one hand from the cockpit. While he was at it, he replaced the original winches with heavy duty upgrades. He installed furling gear for the mainsail as well as the headsail, in order to avoid the cumbersome (and often dangerous) business of lowering and tying sails in a tossing sea. He all but took apart the auxiliary diesel engine, tinkering with her until she purred to his satisfaction.

"Where will you be taking her?" I asked. Given the amount of work he'd been putting into her, nothing would have shocked me.

"Don't know yet," Jack confessed. "But I've always wanted to go on a *real* sail. Not just island-hopping for a week. A *trip,* y'know?"

He did all of the work himself. On those occasions when I helped, or when my son and I both pitched in, it was always quite clear that Jack was in charge of the operation and that we were there to follow his directions and be guided by his specifications.

That's why it came as something of a surprise to me when Jack invited me to join him on whatever journey it was that he was preparing for.

"So," he said one afternoon, "you want to come along?" As simple as that.

It turned out that "along" was to be a voyage of some 1,500 miles, the final leg of it a 600-mile stretch in the open waters of the Atlantic. The destination was to be a tiny dot of land rising out of the sea, formed by the overgrown tip of a long-dormant volcano. It was named Walker Island, after (or so Jack told me) its discoverer, the explorer John Ransom Walker, who two years later would die in a storm off the much larger Bermuda Islands, in roughly the same longitude but several hundred miles to the north. Jack had been planning the trip ever since the doctors confirmed his diagnosis. It was something he'd always secretly wanted to do but had always put off. Now the time seemed suddenly right. He was determined to do it while he still had the strength, before the inevitable downward spiral began taking its toll on his body. And he was prepared to do it alone, if need be.

"But I'd sure love to have company," he said, smiling and looking me square in the eye. He confessed that his list of acceptable crew members was somewhat on the short side: Mine was the only name on it.

"I've got a wife and three kids," I reminded him, "not to mention a law practice. I'll have to think about it." But even as I left him at the boatyard that afternoon, I knew full well that he'd made me the offer of a lifetime. My only brother, my best friend on the planet, figured he had one great adventure left in his life, and now he was asking me to share it with him.

What kind of a choice was that?

2

W e worked on the boat into late winter, gradually transforming her from a recreational day-sailer to an ocean-going cruiser. While others huddled around fireplaces and waited for snows to melt, we lowered her into the water and began testing her in the February winds and whitecaps, learning how to compensate for all the modifications we'd made. With the added weight in her keel, we found she could take more canvas. Where once she'd had difficulty sailing close to the wind, now she could point smartly. We took her out in the rain to see how tight her fittings were, then in choppy seas to discover what needed to be lashed down. We tore sails, broke hatch covers, and lost gear overboard. But, day by day, we learned, and the boat never once let us down.

By early March, we began provisioning her, laying in whatever supplies we thought we might possibly need for a voyage that could find us at sea for as long as three months. Food was not our biggest concern: While the amount of fresh fruits and vegetables we could take was limited by how fast things would spoil, we knew we had ample room aboard for a good year's worth of cans and dry goods. It was water that we worried about, Jack had ripped out one of the berths to add extra tanks, which we filled for washing and showering; for drinking and cooking, we spent a small fortune on huge plastic containers meant for water-coolers, and broke our backs lugging them aboard and wedging them into places where they were least likely to come free and bounce around.

We loaded safety gear and spare parts, repair manuals and hand tools. We fought over how high-tech we were willing to be in terms of navigation. Radar, loran, and Sat-Nav were ruled out, since we were determined to do our own positioning and plotting. But we did opt for some fairly sophisticated radio equipment that would enable us to receive weather reports when we'd be well out of range of onshore stations.

By mid-March, Jack had quit his job, and he spent almost every day at the marina, scraping and sanding, painting and polishing. I'd join him on weekends, and we'd spend mornings going over inventory, stowing and restowing gear, checking every system and every backup system. Afternoons, when the breezes picked up, we'd take her out of the harbor and into the bay, leaning her into whatever wind we could find, driving her against the biggest waves in sight, all the while fine-tuning her rigging and our own abilities.

Then one evening, back on the shore after a grueling series of hard tacks and jibes in six-foot seas and freezing rain, Jack turned to me and said, "I think we're ready." I wasn't sure if he meant the two of us, or was counting the boat as well, but - cold and wet beyond caring - I simply nodded in agreement.

We wanted to leave early in the year - not so early that the days would still be short when we sailed the islands of local waters, but early enough to reach our destination, turn around, and be safely back before late summer and the beginning of hurricane season. Now we told our loved ones that our window of opportunity was but a few short weeks away.

Jack spent those weeks with his daughters, seeing as much of them as their school schedules permitted. The divorce had driven some distance between them, as the girls had rallied to their mother's side over what they'd perceived at the time as their father's abandonment of her. The closeness that Jack had shared with them would never be entirely restored, but his trip to New England was Jack's way of both making amends and asking forgiveness.

I took leave of the law, spending those last weeks ashore with my wife and our three children, torn between how terribly I'd miss them over the coming months and the irresistible pull of the adventure I was about to undertake. To their credit, my family understood this pull, and if they thought of the trip as some foolish midlife crisis, they never said so to my face.

At the boatyard one evening, Jack painted over the faded lettering that had graced the stern of the boat since before he'd bought it. We wanted to rename her after some sleek creature of the sea, and at one time or another we'd considered *Dolphin, Porpoise, Barracuda,* and *Amberjack.* But as we were buying fish from a local market at the end of one day, Jack and I came across a package of unappetizing-looking imitation crabmeat that some marketing euphemist had labeled "sea legs" in a burst of optimism. We looked at each other and grinned. Neither of us spoke a word - it was like that between my brother and me. But our boat had its new name.

The day of our departure dawned bright and clear and unseasonably warm, and we were joined by a throng of well-wishers at the dock. There were toasts and speeches, hugs and kisses, tears and pledges. Jack's ex-wife pulled me aside at one point and held my eyes with hers.

"Promise me you'll both come back safely," she said.

And of course I promised.

Finally, Jack fired up the diesel. I sounded three short blasts on the air horn, and we dropped our land lines and shoved off. With Jack at the wheel, I took up a spot near the bow, from where I could look back and watch those who continued to wave from shore grow smaller and smaller, until they disappeared completely.

We motored out of the marina and into the harbor before raising our sails. There comes a moment in sailing unlike anything else I know, a single instant so precious and intense that it never passes without producing a sense of total reverence in me. It is that moment when, with sails newly raised and trimmed, the engine is killed. Suddenly, the mechanical drone that has filled the air gives way to the silent sounds of the sea - the slapping of wind against canvas and water against hull, and the wonderful groan of the boat as it strains to surge forward under the same power that has propelled man over the waves throughout the ages.

I made my way back to the cockpit and took up a position next to Jack, so that we stood shoulder-to-shoulder at the wheel. We'd been the same height since he'd caught up sometime during our teens. At this point I outweighed him by a good ten or fifteen pounds, but people sometimes asked if we were twins. The truth was that I was nearly three years older than Jack. Once those years had seemed a significant gap, and it struck me that Jack had spent much of his early life trying to bridge it. He'd played harder, studied longer, and worked more diligently than I. He'd discovered girls earlier, taken up cigarettes, and even grown a beard - all (he'd confessed to me years later) in a determined effort to close whatever distance our births had placed between us. By now, perhaps through his sheer will (or, more likely, as a simple result of our inevitable passage into adulthood), he'd succeeded.

"I'm glad you came," Jack said softly, without taking his eyes off the mark we were aiming for.

"Me, too," I said, putting a hand on his shoulder.

Touching wasn't something that came easily for Jack and me. We had a mother who, I'm quite convinced, loved us dearly. But she'd never been one to show her affection, and her sons had suffered as a result. Finally, well into our thirties, Jack had driven over one night when his marriage was falling apart, and we sat by a fire, talking until the sun came up, and we were all talked out. "You know, Joe," he'd said, "we never hug each other." And he'd been right, of course. So we'd stood and hugged. It seemed a little awkward at the time, but it felt good, too, and we'd been doing it since. Still, we weren't natural-born huggers, the way some people are; our intimacy lay elsewhere.

We sailed until dusk that first day, following the shoreline before putting in at an anchorage well out of the way of coastal traffic. With the sun down and no clouds to trap the warm air of the afternoon, the temperature dropped sharply. I heated up some homemade soup someone had brought down to the dock that morning, and the aroma of broth and vegetables filled the cabin. But when I offered a mug of it to Jack, he shook his head.

"You know me," he said. "I'll be over the rail most of the night as it is."

And I remember: Jack, who loved the motion of a boat under sail as much as I, fell victim to seasickness at anchor. One might think that fact alone would be enough to keep a man ashore. But I'm a rock climber who's afraid of heights, and I've got an actor friend who suffers from a terrible case of stage fright. Jack would deal with his problem, though not with the aid of pills or patches; he preferred to tough it out all that first night "over the rail," as he put it. After that, he knew he'd be okay the rest of the way. I guess you could say Jack earned his sea legs the hard way, as he did so many things.

3

W e spent the first week or so sailing just offshore, working our way gradually down the coast. We'd wake early, when the morning air was still cold enough that we could see our breath in the first light that filtered into the cabin. We'd fire up the stove and start a pot of coffee, then climb back into our sleeping bags while it brewed.

When you're at anchor in the lee of the mainland, the wind dies down considerably at night, and an early start is generally a sluggish one. We found it better to wait until the sun was well up before setting out each day. So we'd lie in our sleeping bags, taking our time over whatever we happened to be having for breakfast. We'd often brew a second pot of coffee. And we'd talk.

If Jack tended to be a better worker and a harder player than I, it was I to whom words came more easily. Perhaps that had always been the case; more likely, lawyering had brought it out in me over the years. Where Jack spoke carefully and sparingly, I'd long since succumbed to the obnoxious occupational hazard of needing to say the same thing two or three times over, in slightly different ways.

But now Jack seemed to loosen up, and on those chilly spring mornings, as we lay in our sleeping bags at anchor, sipping strong black coffee and waiting for the breeze to freshen, it was Jack who did most of the talking, and I who became the listener.

He talked of his childhood, and how he'd never quite felt like one of the family. For one thing, he hadn't *looked* the same as the rest of us. My dark hair favored that of both our parents while Jack had been almost blond early on, and later sandy-haired. Where my coarse looks closely resembled my father's, and many claimed to see my mother's smile in mine, Jack's narrower face and finer features set him apart. Even his eyes were different: Ours were brown while his were a bluish green.

Growing up, I'd teased Jack that he was adopted, and though he'd pretty much known it wasn't so, every once in a while I'd come up with some shred of evidence to start him worrying all over again: a baby book of mine, but none for him; a photo of me with our parents, with him nowhere in sight, or the family collection of monogrammed napkin rings (a silly fancy in those days), mine in the same style as our parents, and his (no doubt added later on) in a slightly different style and printing. Then he'd run to our mother, sobbing (real tears at first, which eventually gave way to mock ones as he grew older) for fear that it was true, that he'd been adopted after all. My mother would do her best to reassure him, and she'd promise solemnly that he'd been born into the family, and Jack would be okay for a bit, until I'd get around to explaining to him that *of course* she'd have to say that, or that she'd probably completely forgotten about his adoption by that time.

One time when we were sitting around the dinner table with our parents, Jack had asked for more whipped cream on his dessert. He *loved* whipped cream and would put it on just about anything: cereal, cantaloupe, even *eggs*. At that moment, he was licking the last of his portion from his plate. "It must be true," I said, "what they put in the report from the adoption agency." All eyes turned to me. "You know," I explained, "the part about his being raised by cats?"

Mornings on the boat, Jack talked about school, and about how for years he'd been known to his teachers as "Joey's brother." Finally, our parents had had the good sense to switch him to a different school, and he'd done well there after a while, though the change was difficult for him at first. If I'd been a hard act for Jack to follow, I'd also been his protector. No one messes with a kid who's got a big brother nearby. So I'd become a mixed blessing for my younger brother: I was his idol, his teacher, and he loved being around me. But I could make his life miserable at times, too.

He talked of how intense his transition from adolescence to young adulthood had been. He'd started smoking when he was ten or eleven, sneaking puffs from some cigarette our mother would leave burning unattended in an ashtray. Occasionally, he'd grow bold enough to steal one from her pack. Then he'd lock himself in the bathroom, and soon I'd hear him running the water or flushing the toilet to cover the sounds of his coughing and choking. "I was determined to become an adult," he explained now, "even if it was going to kill me."

It struck me that I'd spent half a lifetime trying to keep from growing up, while all along Jack had desperately been trying to get there.

His precocious interest in girls had been part of the pattern. In my shyness, I'd hidden behind a pose of superiority and self-sufficiency. "Who needs em?" I'd say, shrugging, while disparaging as "queers" those of my friends who learned to dance. Jack, on the other hand, discovered girls with a vengeance. Perhaps he seized a playing field I'd left to him by default. Or maybe he intuitively recognized that it would one day be a relationship with a girl that would be his ticket out of a family where he so strongly felt the sting of unfair competition. Whatever it was, beginning in his early teens, he fell for one girl after another; each time he fell, he fell hard.

"Do you remember being in love for the very first time?" he asked me now. But as I began to search my memory, Jack barely paused between thoughts, and I quickly realized that his had been a question that needed no answer. *"God!"* he shouted, recalling some young girl from long ago, whose name I can no longer summon but whose memory was clearly burned in my brother's heart forever. "I thought the sheer intensity of it might kill me. Every time we were separated, I cried myself to sleep until I was afraid my heart would give out. I was absolutely, totally convinced that we were the only two people who had ever felt like that." He described making fumbling love with her in the backseat of a car he was too young to drive, in those simpler, long-ago days when getting caught or getting a girl pregnant were the worst things that could possibly happen to a boy.

He talked of a series of such infatuations, each one as consuming as the one before it and the one that would follow it. These were no locker-room boasts on Jack's part; they weren't recounted out of some sense of bravado. They said less about his prowess than they did about his passion - how he'd grown up with this burning, consuming need to love and be loved, and, above all, *to be in love.*

One morning, he told me about meeting the woman who later became his wife. It was a story I'd never heard; for some reason, Jack and his wife had always kept it their secret, even after the love had been wrung out of their marriage, and they'd agreed to go their separate ways. Had it begun with the same sort of passion as the others?

"At first." Jack nodded, his eyes clouding over. I was older then, after all, almost twenty! I was off at college, living off campus in a big old rooming house. I was mowing lawns and splitting firewood in exchange for a free room. Another student dropped out of school and moved out, and the landlady ran an ad in the local paper to fill the empty room, and she asked me to show it to anyone who called to see it.

"One evening, this sophomore transfer student came by. She'd just had a fight with her roommate or something and had stormed out of her dorm. I showed her the room; she didn't think much of it. But she was gorgeous. I couldn't take my eyes off her. Somehow, I got her to sit down, and we started talking. We must have talked for *hours.* By the time we looked at a clock, it was way past midnight, and her dorm was locked for the night. She started making phone calls, trying to find someone to put her up for the night. God, how I prayed that she wouldn't be able to reach anybody!

"So I put on my sincerest voice, swore to the purity of my intentions, and managed to convince her to stay. I let her have my room; I took the unmade bed in the empty one. I gave her my pajama tops to sleep in; I wore the bottoms. For the next hour, I tried my hardest to fall asleep. But it was no use: All I could do was picture her lying in my bed, wearing my pajama tops, and listen to my heart pounding. Finally, I tiptoed down the hallway and stood outside her door, holding my breath. To this day, I don't know what I intended to do next. But I couldn't have been there fifteen seconds when the door slowly started to open, and there she was, getting ready to come down the hall to look for me.

"She never left. We spent the night together, and all the next morning. We ate peanut butter sandwiches on Ritz crackers. It was all I had. We cut whatever classes we were supposed to go to. In the afternoon, we got out of bed long enough to move her stuff in. We were married that June."

"And the passion?" I asked. "Did it continue?"

"For a while," Jack said. "But, you know, it was *okay* when my heart finally stopped pounding. Living on the edge all the time was just too exhausting, too intense. There were simply too many ups and downs, too much anguish, too much jealousy. After we were married awhile, it became different. I began to feel for the first time that I could go to a party and not have to worry about who my date was talking to. I could fall asleep at night, and this person would still be there when I woke up in the morning. It felt *safe*, somehow."

"You were pretty young to get married," I reminded him.

"Yeah, you tried to tell me that." He smiled. "But I wasn't about to listen. I was convinced I was wise beyond my years.

And besides, I needed to prove that I was just as grown-up as you were."

That, of course, had been one of the dominant themes of Jack's early years. "You were awfully rough on me, Joe," he now confided. "You always could do everything better."

"I was almost three years older than you."

"Easy for you to say. But try to imagine what it's like to grow up in someone's shadow, every day of your life, for twenty years."

"You sound like you think I rubbed your nose in it."

"You did!" he pounced. "Not always. But you had your moments. Hey" - he smiled a little ruefully - "you must have loved being better at things every bit as much as I hated being worse. How could you not?"

"Sorry," I mumbled.

"You know, I can still remember the first time I ever beat you at something," he said, and I knew what was coming before he told me, because I remembered it, too. "We'd both been in some stupid Ping-Pong tournament one summer when we were away on vacation somewhere. And we'd both gotten all the way to the finals. I must have been ten, so I guess you were thirteen. I wanted to beat you in the worst way. So help me, I can still remember some of the *points,* some of the shots I made. And I did it - somehow I beat you. And as soon as it was over, you told me you had let me win."

I didn't remember that part. "I lied," I confessed now. "I played my best. But I guess it must have been too hard for me to let you know that."

"But don't you see what you did? For a moment, I was on top of the world. You took it all away from me when you said that. Don't you *see* that?"

"I do *now*," I said. "I was thirteen, remember."

"How about *me,* Joe? I was *ten,* for God's sake."

On the tenth day, we motored into a marina, which would be our last stop before turning cast and leaving the mainland behind us. Though we both preferred lying at anchor to spending the night tied up in a slip, we decided to make an exception that evening.

We took on water and fuel, knowing it would be our last chance to top up our tanks. We bought fresh fruits and vegetables, two commodities you never have enough of in a small boat at sea. We found a Laundromat to do our wash, and a pay phone to call family and friends. We took showers ashore without having to worry about how much hot water we were using. Then we sat down for dinner in a restaurant, complete with menus and wine lists and tablecloths and waiters - something we knew we wouldn't get to do for another two months.

When we got back aboard *Sea Legs,* however, we were kept awake by noises coming from other boats, and by the odor of diesel fumes indigenous to marinas everywhere. The combination of the two was enough to drive us from our slip. We untied our land lines, motored out in the darkness, and dropped anchor well out in the harbor. There, the only sounds and smells to reach us were those of the sea herself.

We realized at that moment that although we stilt lay in the shadow of the mainland, our hearts had already cast off from it.

In the morning, an offshore breeze came up early. We raised our sails while still at anchor, so as to avoid the noise and needless bother of the motor. As I pulled the hook free at the bow, Jack worked in the cockpit, pulling in the sheets at exactly the right moment to catch the breeze. The sails stiffened and filled, as though they, too, were eager to get under way. Slowly at first, then more and more surely, we left our anchorage behind us, picking up speed as we traded the protection of the harbor for the vast expanse of water ahead. We pointed due east, away from shore, away at last from dry land, toward a tiny speck of land in the middle of nowhere. Ours was the very first boat on the water that morning, and to me it seemed as though we were the only two men alive on the face of the earth.

Sometime before noon, we saw the sea beneath us gradually change from the familiar green and aqua shades of coastal waters to the deep majestic blue of open ocean.

4

When I think back now to what I felt that morning, the single word that keeps coming to mind is *exhilaration*. I was doing what I loved as much as anything in the world, and I was doing it with the person who'd been my best friend for all his life and nearly all of mine. We were heading east, into a sun whose warmth reached out to welcome us, and whose reflection on the water dazzled our eyes with its brilliance.

Never mind that neither of us had ever really been to sea before. Forget that open-water navigation was something we'd only studied in books, or that we'd soon be completely at the mercy of whatever weather the sea chose to test us with. That morning, I felt superhuman, absolutely invincible. Quite literally, for as far as the eye could see, there was nothing ahead of us but dazzling sunshine, crystal-clear sky, and blue ocean.

But if dazzling sunshine produces exhilaration, it can also lead to blindness. I let myself take for granted that the broad smile on Jack's face signified that his thoughts perfectly mirrored my own. And I'm sure I was right, up to a point. But I now know that much more must have been going on in Jack's mind that morning, and that to him, the glorious spectacle laid out before us must have taken on a different meaning altogether.

I knew none of that then, of course: While I felt the exhilaration, I never sensed the blindness. All I knew was that we were off on the adventure of our lives, my brother and I, and at that moment, it seemed that nothing could possibly stand in our way.

One of the differences between island-hopping and open-water sailing is the need for charting a course. When you're in sight of land, it's sufficient to sail by "eyeball navigation," simply progressing from visible point to visible point - connecting the dots, so to speak. This method will often do even when the distance between points is such that you find yourself out of sight of both points on occasion: If the land masses are close enough, or large enough, the next one will invariably pop into view ahead of you, so long as you pay a minimum of attention to the compass or even the position of the sun.

Ocean navigation is a different matter altogether. Gone are the landmarks: There are no buoys at sea, no markers for the uncertain traveler. Blue-water sailing is as different from coastal sailing as crossing a desert is from traveling city streets.

Just as I became the keeper of the log aboard *Sea Legs* by default, I also became her navigator. It fell to me to plot our course on chart after chart that showed nothing but open water. Under Jack's watchful eye, I'd aim the sextant and take shots of the sun several times each day and of the stars each night, measuring the distance in degrees from the horizon.

Then I'd get out the conversion tables and try to figure out our position, marking it on the chart.

By keeping a constant eye on our speed indicator, and compensating for tides and sideways drifting, I'd do my best to approximate our position between bearing checks - the business of dead reckoning. At first, I was wildly erratic. I'd figure either too much progress or too little; I'd fail to sufficiently compensate for drifting or I'd overcompensate. But after a while, I became quite good at it, and eventually I got to the point where I had few or no corrections to make after checking with the sextant. Then I'd boast to Jack of my newly acquired skill, and he'd nod approvingly, as though he were the older brother and I the youngster.

I was content to think that's all there was to this reversal of our lifelong roles: Jack was finally captain, and I mate. I thrilled to the new order of things, imagining how very satisfying it had to be for Jack finally to find himself in the role of teacher - to the very one in whose shadow he'd suffered for so long.

Foolishly, I was seeing only the obvious; once again, I was completely missing what must have been going on beneath the surface.

Yet the biggest difference that first day out wasn't the vast expanse of ocean spread out before us, or my first clumsy attempts at open-water navigation, or the perceptibly bigger waves and swells we felt beneath us, or even the fact that we now seldom saw another boat on the horizon. The biggest difference was this: As afternoon turned to evening, and evening to night, instead of being able to duck into some protected cove in search of a comfortable anchorage, we flicked on our running lights, zipped up our jackets, and plunged on into the darkness.

For me, this was a new experience, and I admit that it took some getting used to. By running lights, I mean the small red and green sidelights our boat was required to carry in order to enable another vessel to see us. As for what we could see, that was a different matter altogether. Unlike a car, a boat has no headlights; the resulting sensation is one of hurtling forward into a solid wall of blackness. Try to imagine sitting in an open roadster, speeding down a deserted country lane on a moonless night, and suddenly turning off the headlights.

To be sure, the analogy is not altogether a fair one: There are no oncoming cars at sea, and no need to stay within the lanes of a narrow strip of pavement. But there can be other vessels out there, huge ships, on whose radar screens a tiny sailboat like ours might not even create a visible blip. And there is all manner of floating or barely submerged debris lying in wait, much of it big enough to rip a small boat's hull apart and send it to the bottom in minutes.

We'd outfitted *Sea Legs* with a self-steering device, a contraption designed to correct the angle of the rudder automatically whenever we strayed off a preset heading. And though we'd tested the device and trusted it up to a point, we weren't about to turn our lives over to it that first night at sea. We stayed together in the cockpit for hours, taking turns at the wheel, steering by the tiny light of the compass. But if Jack was as frightened as I was, he never showed it. While I nervously scanned the horizon for lights and listened for distant engines, my brother wore the wry grin of a seasoned mariner, ready to do battle with whatever dragons might be out there.

"Relax, Joe," he told me more than once, amused at my fretting.

"I can't help it," I confessed. "I like living."

"Me, too," he said, smiling. "But this is living. This is something I've always imagined doing. It used to frighten me in my dreams - heading into the unknown. But then I got to the point where I learned to trust that it would be okay. A nightmare turns into an amusement-park ride as soon as you know it's going to have a happy ending."

I tried my best to see it Jack's way. I concentrated on everything that was positive about our situation. The wind had fallen off a bit with the coming of night. Whereas during the day, we'd been heading almost due east, now we turned a bit to the south, so as to have the breeze over one shoulder, lessening the likelihood of an accidental boom-swinging jibe. The result was a comfortable ride over gentle swells, with a minimum of heeling. The night air was cold, but, with the collars of our heavy jackets turned up, we stayed warm and dry. With only a crescent of a moon showing, the sky filled with a riot of stars. It truly didn't get any prettier than this anyplace on earth.

I told myself that the blackness in front of us wasn't really a solid wall that we were about to crash into, after all. I recalled sailing in fog so thick that the visibility had actually been far less. Here at least, in the clear air ahead, we'd see the lights of another ship in time to react.

Jack did his part by trying to distract me with conversation. We talked of our earliest memories, of school and summer camp. We recalled the names of teachers and counselors, of fellow students and campers I hadn't thought of for thirty years or more. We conjured up distant relatives, long dead and buried. We retold stories of incidents so old that we remembered the stories but not the incidents themselves, such as the time we'd been sitting in my father's car and one of us had pushed in the cigarette lighter and removed it when it had popped out. We'd then proceeded to take turns burning our hands, passing the glowing lighter back and forth like a hot potato, all the while wailing in pain, afraid that if we dropped it, we'd set the car on fire. Or the time we'd come upon a deserted cabin deep in the woods, climbed up a ladder to the attic, and accidentally knocked over a nest of yellow jackets.

What a history we shared. It formed the basis of an intimacy that my own wife learned to grow jealous of in time. Lying beside me in bed, she'd suddenly turn to me. "Talk to me about when you were a child," she'd say, "like you always do with Jack." And I'd try. But it was no use; my roots were so deeply entangled with Jack's that when it came to competing with him in revisiting my past, she never had a chance.

Eventually, we grew weary of remembering and reliving our youth, and we listened to the sounds of the sea and the slapping of wind against canvas. Even in silence, Jack and I were able to communicate. Growing up so close for so many years had created a bond between us, a bond unlike any other I've ever known. Our relationship required no words. It seemed I always knew Jack's thoughts, and he mine, though I know how foolish that must sound.

And bit by bit that night, I felt the fear begin to slip away, and the blackness in front of me eventually take on a depth it hadn't seemed to possess at first.

After a while, Jack went below and put together some dinner We ate at the wheel. I can no longer remember just what it was we had, but the meal made me recall a memory of cooking over a campfire with my father and Jack long ago, grilling landlocked salmon we'd just pulled out of a mountain lake, and swearing that no meal had ever tasted so good.

It was well after midnight before I became accustomed enough to night-sailing to allow Jack to go below and get some sleep. What it took, finally, was Jack's explanation of how *he* dealt with the possibility that we might hit something. "Sure there's a chance," he agreed. "But it's just too slim to worry about. Anyway, there's nothing we can do about it. It's kind of like getting struck by lightning - I'm not going to bother worrying about that, either."

Lightning?

Jack relieved me at the wheel after an hour or two, and I went below. Sleeping aboard a small sailboat at sea is tricky business. At anchor, you bob up and down regularly, and the boat traces gentle arcs, back and forth, rocking you to sleep. Under sail, you can find yourself heeling steeply to one side or the other, rising and falling erratically on waves and swells, yawing suddenly in either direction, and experiencing sudden changes in both speed and direction of travel. But this, too, I got used to after a bit, and the sleep that finally came seemed doubly refreshing because it felt as though I'd *earned* it.

It was still dark when I rejoined Jack in the cockpit. We sat together without speaking. Not long after, we watched the blackness in front of us turn first to midnight blue, then navy, proceeding through an infinite progression of lighter and lighter blues. Then the blue turned to violet, to pink, then to glowing red. Dead ahead, a sun of molten orange broke from the horizon and proclaimed that we'd made it through our first night at sea.

"God, it's good to be alive," Jack said.

"You can say *that* again."

"God, it's good to be alive," he repeated.

I could have told you he'd do that.

For me, those first weeks at sea with Jack were perhaps the very happiest time of my life, before or since. In my short lifetime, I've fallen in love and married, I've seen my three children come into the world healthy, I've won courtroom victories that seemed all but unwinnable, and I've had novels published against lottery odds. But none of those experiences, as wonderful as they all were, provided me with quite the same sense of sustained euphoria as did those weeks of getting to know my brother all over again.

There were occasions when I'd catch myself watching Jack for long stretches of time - as he manned the wheel, or trimmed the sails, or attended to some little chore that needed looking after. Jack had a certain grace about him, an economy of motion I more often associate with an animal in the wild. There was no fat on him: He was lean to the point of being wiry, but he was strong and athletically fit. Deeply tanned by now, he took on a healthy glow that made it hard for me to remember that, somewhere inside, he was ill. At work, he possessed an adult's steady hand and confident smile; yet there was always a child's sense of awe and mirth lurking just beneath the surface, ready to erupt without a moment's notice.

I think I loved life as a young man as much as most. I saw now how Jack *reveled* in life, how he drank in every moment of it. Each sunrise, each sunset, each appearance of the moon and stars moved him close to tears. A flying fish soaring across our bow brought an ovation from him. The sight of a whale breaching to starboard stamped a daylong grin on his face.

One afternoon, a pod of dolphins decided to escort us through the waves.

"Stop her! Stop her!" Jack shouted, and, stripping off his shirt and sneakers, he promptly dove headfirst over the rail and out of sight. Frantically, I strove to rein in *Sea Legs*. But having no brakes, a sailboat slows only by losing momentum once the canvas is let loose, and so it must have taken me a full quarter of a mile to bring us dead in the water. When finally I regained sight of Jack, he was bobbing well back in our wake, waving his arms and crying out in what I first took to be distress. I threw him the horseshoe buoy and was searching about in desperation for a line to fling his way, when I realized he was laughing hysterically.

"They *carried* me!" he shouted over and over as I dragged him back aboard. "They took turns *carrying* me on their *noses!*"

He laughed for hours. For days, he laughed.

Another day, as we were changing sails to compensate for increasing winds, one of us let go of a halyard - the line used to raise and lower a sail - and before we knew it the shackle was swinging up by the top of the mast, some thirty feet above our heads.

"I'll get my harness," I said. I'd brought along some of my rock-climbing gear for just such a moment. I'd tried to teach Jack climbing a couple of times, and he could've been good at it. His wiry frame, agility, and determination made him well equipped. But he'd never really taken to it - "Not all that crazy about heights" is how he put it if I remember correctly. So when I emerged from below with a harness and a couple of carabiners, I was surprised to see Jack reaching for them.

"I got it," I told him.

"No way!" Jack laughed, taking the harness from me and stepping into it. "This could be the scariest thing of all time!" So we clipped him onto a spare halyard and leaving the piloting to the self-steering device, I winched him up the mast.

Understand that all the while we were making close to ten knots in seas rough enough to have caused us to want to reduce sails in the first place. Things were plenty tricky on deck, down where I was. Thirty feet above, the tip of the mast pendulumed wildly with each wave so that Jack, clinging to it, swung back and forth in a giant arc. One moment he'd be straight overhead, the next well out over the water, but never was he in one spot for more than an instant.

So I can't say I was too surprised when I heard his first scream. But I knew I had a good belay on him and that there was no way he could fall.

"Hang on!" I shouted. "I've got you good!"

But I needn't have worried; it took me only a moment to realize that, once again, my brother wasn't in the grip of terror so much as in the throes of ecstasy. His screams (which he kept up the whole time he was aloft) were mixed with laughter. They were the screams of a kid who's just discovered what life is like in the front seat of a roller coaster.

At some point, I managed to remind Jack he was up there to do a job, and finally he gathered in the shackle and let me lower him, still laughing, back to the relative calm of the deck.

Yet all afternoon I caught him eyeing the top of the mast, and at any moment I fully expected him to demand a re-ride.

Why do I go to such great lengths here to recount these foolish antics of my brother? Why do I dwell so now - some fifteen years later - to paint this portrait of Jack those first few weeks at sea aboard *Sea Legs?* The answer is this: In all of our years together, I'd simply never seen Jack so happy, so animated, so absolutely *full of life.* The pure joy I took in watching him defies all description; at times, it seemed to me so absolutely intense as to border on pain.

Oh, to be frozen in time! To be able to go back to some singular moment and place in the past and dwell there forever - immune to the rest of the world, safe from the future. I not only know now, with hindsight, what my choice would be; so help me, I knew it *then.*

5

There comes an entry in *The Log of the Sea Legs* that is shorter than any other. It is a single sentence on a page that contains nothing else but a date and our position on the ocean. There are no entries of any sort for the three days that followed.

For fifteen years, I've seen that page, that sentence, in my mind's eye. More than any other - more than all the others combined - it was that one entry that had kept me from the attic all those fifteen years. Even when I finally climbed the stairs and opened the trunk and found what I was looking for, it was that entry which lowered me to the floor and kept me from opening the book until my hands would stop trembling.

When at last I forced my fingers to begin the process of turning the pages, I drew inexorably closer to the source of my dread, until I began to feel that the paper itself was taking on a *heat,* and I actually came to imagine that when I turned to *that* page, *that* entry, the paper might literally ignite in my hands.

It didn't, of course. I reached the page and saw the entry. There was no combustion, no spontaneous conflagration. After a while, I was even able to read the words themselves without the blood pounding deafeningly in my ears.

Seven words. Seven benign little words. Thirty-two letters, set apart by six spaces, ending with a period. Nothing more, nothing less: *Today Jack told me about Walker Island.*

"So why Walker Island?" I asked one evening as we sat below, leaving the piloting to the self-steering device for a bit "Whatever made you decide on that for a destination?"

"Because it's there," Jack answered, the way a mountain climber brushes off his need to tackle a particular peak.

"So's Bermuda," I said.

"Too built-up. They make you wear leather shoes and black socks there. They've got paved streets and traffic lights, and all the other things that ruin islands."

"And Walker?"

"Coconuts and bananas, mangoes that ripen on the tree. Wild sugarcane. Sea turtles that come ashore in the full moon to lay their eggs in black volcanic sand. Crawfish the size of lobsters. Rainbow-colored birds seen nowhere else on the planet."

"That's all?"

"I think there's a Burger King, too."

By now, we were making good progress east-southeast, averaging better than eight knots during the day, and close to five at night. We'd fallen into a routine that permitted us to alternate regular turns at the wheel, attend to such chores as cooking and cleaning, or grab a few hours of sleep. But the sum of those activities accounted for only about half of our time, leaving the remaining hours free.

Invariably, we chose to spend those free hours together, either in conversation or comfortable silence. When you're with someone you love in the fullest sense of the word - someone you've come to know as well as you know yourself - long periods of quiet become every bit as acceptable as long stretches of talk, sometimes even more so. With Jack and me, there was never a need to fill time with words. Silence bore no price tag; quiet came free of guilt.

It helped, no doubt, that we were doing something we both loved to do, and that we were doing it in a setting so beautiful, so profoundly majestic, that there were times when to speak was to break the spell.

Each day brought glorious panoramas of sun, sky, and sea. As we progressed farther south - and as late April gave way to early May - the afternoons grew increasingly warmer, and often we stripped down to shorts by midday. There were times we saw clouds, to be sure, but they were either far off or high above us, and for the most part thin and white. Several days we sailed through showers, but none of them lasted long enough to bother us.

Evening brought its own version of beauty. Early on, we were treated to incredible displays of stars. We identified every constellation in the sky, every planet visible to the naked eye. We counted shooting stars until we could count no more.

Night by night, the moon swelled toward full, but not without exacting its own price: Nightly, we lost stars by the hundreds, by the thousands, and we went weeks without sighting a single shooting star. But the price turned out to be a small one indeed, for now each night we were treated to a moonlit ocean for as far as the eye could see. On the water, every swell came to life; every crest reflected the moon in a million shattered pieces. Flying fish became tiny rockets launched from wave to wave. Hordes of iridescent minnows, jellyfish, and sea worms parted to make room for our bow. The blackness before us - that same blackness to which I'd ascribed an imaginary depth early on - now gave way to a welcoming blue that stretched all the way to a visible horizon.

Night became a magical time for Jack and me aboard *Sea Legs*, a time to huddle together in the warmth of her cockpit, or to stand riding upon her prow - the wind stinging our faces, the sea spray matting our hair, the ocean rhythmically rising and falling beneath us - watching miracles unfold before our eyes.

By now, I'd marked our progress across several charts that showed nothing but open water, and we were reaching the point where, as navigator, I needed to know the exact position of our destination. According to what Jack had told me, if we missed Walker Island, there was simply nothing beyond it but ocean. The next landfall at our latitude would be the western coast of North Africa, some 2,500 miles away. As good a time as I was having aboard *Sea Leg*s, that wasn't a mistake I wanted to make.

So one day, as I neared the eastern edge of the chart I was using, I asked Jack to find me the next one I'd need. "And while you're at it, you might as well give me the rest of them. It's time we began thinking about our approach."

"We're weeks away," Jack said.

"I know." I nodded. "Still, I'd like to start getting us lined up."

He disappeared below. But when he came back up a few minutes later, he had only the next chart in sequence. "The rest of them are wrapped separately - in plastic," he explained. "I'll open them up later and get you what you need." And with that, he turned away and busied himself with some chore or other.

Now the thing was, Jack never could lie to me. Perhaps that's always the case with a younger brother; who knows? I do know that, beginning with the time when we were kids, Jack's every attempt at deception was as transparent to me as air itself.

I remember once misplacing a baseball bat, a brand-new thirty-two ounce Gene Woodling Louisville Slugger. A week later, I noticed Jack using an identical model - only his looked old and dirty. I grabbed it from him and began inspecting it, ready to accuse him of larceny. "Hey!" he complained. "That's mine! It's even got my *name* on it." And so it did. There was his *JACK*, freshly engraved with a wood- burning set of the very type our father kept in the drawer of his workbench. As for the dirt, it came free with the rub of a cloth. In a moment of uncharacteristic charity, I let Jack off the hook. I told him he could keep the bat, provided he let me borrow it whenever I was up. But both of us knew from that moment on that he'd never be able to get anything past me.

Another time, in our early teens, *Playboy* magazines began arriving mysteriously, once a month, at our home. The label bore our last name, preceded only by the initial J., a clue that only narrowed it down to Jack, my father, and me. Jack swore up and down that he was innocent, and I think he may have convinced my parents, who no doubt considered him too young to be interested in such things. But once a month for a full year, my brother found it absolutely impossible to look me in the eye without dissolving into confessional laughter. There were lots of things Jack could do. Lying to me just didn't happen to be one of them.

That's why I so easily rejected Jack's excuse about the remaining charts being wrapped in plastic - and why he didn't even press the point when I asked him about it a day or two later.

We were running wing and wing at the time, though why I remember that now, I can't say. The wind was directly behind us, coming over our stern and pushing us along in an efficient, if unexciting, manner. To take advantage of the conditions, we'd let the boom swing well out over the starboard side and had coaxed the jib all the way out to port. The result was a great expanse of sail, set almost perpendicular to the wind, our version of the balloon-like spinnaker often flown by bigger boats running downwind.

"So what's the deal with Walker Island?" I asked.

I don't know precisely what I expected in the way of an answer. Maybe that Jack would admit we were heading for Africa after all, or the Canary Islands, just off its coast. Or perhaps he'd tell me again about the coconuts and bananas, the mangoes that ripened on the trees, the wild sugarcane, the sea turtles, the black volcanic sand, the crawfish the size of lobsters, and the rainbow-colored birds seen nowhere else on the planet. But I was pretty certain of one thing: He wouldn't lie to me. He knew better than that.

Still, I wasn't prepared for what he *did* say.

And now, as I sit over my typewriter fifteen years later, I can still hear my brother's words as though they'd been spoken this very moment. They ring in my ears to this day. They will echo in my mind forever.

"There is no Walker Island" is what Jack said.

6

In trying to re-create the effect of Jack's statement on me some fifteen years after the fact, I realize that, at the time I heard his words, I experienced such a tremendous onslaught of emotions that it's difficult for me to sort them out now and place them in any precise, meaningful sequence.

At first, I suppose, I must have thought he was joking, that he'd succumbed to his occasional flair for the melodramatic. I waited for some tale of how our destination had mysteriously disappeared off the charts, some *Twilight Zone* account involving interrupted radio transmissions and unconfirmed sightings of giant whirlpools that our government refused to confirm but couldn't deny. But no tale came.

I expected an announcement that we were going to try to make it clear across the Atlantic in our thirty-six-foot boat, in search of a place in the history books, or at the bottom of the ocean. But no announcement followed.

I was thoroughly, hopelessly confused; something was going on, yet I had absolutely no clue what it was. I felt stupid for failing to catch on and negligent for not having studied up on our destination on my own. I also felt seriously betrayed: Jack had told me about one plan, and now it was apparent that all the while he'd had something else in mind.

But as upsetting as all those feelings were, none of them (indeed, not all of them combined) rose to the level of being deeply disturbing. And yet I remember how deeply, how profoundly disturbed I began to feel as I struggled to make sense of what Jack had just told me.

I suppose the single word that most comes to mind now is *dread*. All Jack had really done was to tell me that we were headed to some place different from the one he'd led me to believe. What was so unnerving about that? My brother had always been full of surprises, for as long as I could remember. Nonetheless, I felt a sense of gathering dread like no other I'd ever felt before or have felt since. The result was that I found myself momentarily immobilized, suspended between curiosity and panic, wanting to know what was going on - where we were heading - and at the same time *not* wanting to know. *Desperately* not wanting to know.

So I readily confess to you that I took the easy way out. I closed my eyes and covered my ears and asked no questions. I sought refuge in the safe harbor of ignorance. And I curled up in my bunk that night and found sleep in the snuggest of all hurricane holes - avoidance.

Students of human behavior tell us that much is to be learned from the ways in which we sleep. Whole laboratories are devoted to the videotaping of sleeping subjects. We are now able to study the tiny electrical impulses that travel through the brain, and in doing so, we've learned much about our unconscious selves. And it is no accident that our language is full of descriptive phrases such as "slept the sleep of the just" or "slept like a baby," in ready contrast to "slept fitfully" or "had a troubled sleep."

I've always tended to sleep sprawled out, splayed across the mattress, my unconscious self apparently determined to fill whatever space there is. My wife long ago learned to stake out a small space for herself in our bed and defend it tenaciously against my incursions.

But that morning, I awoke, disoriented, to find myself clenched into a fetal ball, drawn in upon myself in some desperation to seal myself off from the world outside. My eyes burned, and my body ached. I felt every bit as tired as I had when I first lay down. I struggled to my feet. I stretched my back and kneaded my muscles to unknot the cramps that had set in during the night. With difficulty, I made my way up the steps to the cockpit.

For the first time, instead of being greeted by a sun that warmed from orange to yellow as it rose from the horizon, I found myself staring into a blood-red sky above our bow.

Jack was already at the wheel, the sun's glow reflected hotly on his face. We exchanged grunts, and I took over for him as he went below to make coffee and see what there was for breakfast.

The whole morning is now nothing more than a blur to me, down the passage of these fifteen years. I must have steered the boat and trimmed the sails; I'm sure we drank coffee, black and strong and sweet, as always; probably we ate, though I cannot recall what it was or how it tasted. I was still involved in the business of avoidance. If there was no Walker Island, I wasn't yet ready to talk about where we *were* going, or what was to happen once we got there.

But avoidance is, for me at least, a difficult exercise. Instead of allowing one to be relaxed and open, avoidance demands effort, concentration, *vigilance.* It is exhausting stuff. By midday, I was worn out, and I retreated once again to the womb of my bunk. There I drifted in and out of sleep. For the first time since we'd been at sea, I dreamt of home.

When finally I forced myself to get up, it wasn't because I was rested; I wasn't. I simply knew that Jack deserved some relief at the wheel. I brushed my teeth, splashed some water on my face, and made my way up the steps.

Emerging from the cabin, I was immediately struck by two things - or, more accurately, by the *absence* of two things.

The first was sunlight.

Sailing in good weather can be a terribly seductive thing. Without realizing it, you soon fall into a rhythm that is so pleasant, it is positively hypnotic. You get so accustomed to bright sun and steady breezes that you can't help being lulled into believing that there'll be no end to them. After a while, you begin to take things for granted, you become sloppy. You don't bother checking the barometer quite so often. You forget to turn on the radio periodically to hunt for a weather report on the shortwave band. The business of sailing becomes so easy, so comfortable - so second nature - that you develop a sense of confidence in your own competence, a feeling that you're in complete control not only over your boat but also over your surroundings.

Now, coming back up on deck, I saw a sky inexplicably filled with clouds. Not the high white wisps that from time to time had brought us relief from the heat, either by filtering the sun's heat or gracing us with an occasional cooling shower. These were thick gray clouds, stretching from the horizon in front of us like a giant carpet being unrolled above our heads. The sun was still visible behind us to the west, but it seemed as though it was in retreat, being crowded out of the sky by the advancing mass.

The second thing that was missing was wind.

Which is an overstatement, to be sure. But we'd enjoyed good winds behind us for so long, the immediate sensation I now felt was that our speed had been cut by half. And I was right. One look at the instruments confirmed that we were making barely four knots, compared with the usual eight or ten we'd grown used to.

"When did this happen?" I asked Jack.

"The pressure began dropping last night," he answered, letting me know that at least one of us had been paying attention. "Notice this morning's sunrise?"

I struggled to remember, but morning seemed ages ago. Sleeping in short bursts has a way of doing that to me.

"Red," Jack reminded me.

And I remembered the sun rising blood red in front of us, its glow reflected hotly on lack's face. And I recalled the ancient rhyme:

Red sun at night,

Mariner's delight.

Red sun at morning,

Mariner's warning.

At the time, I'd noticed only the beauty; Jack had read the message.

While I took the wheel, Jack went below and tried to find a weather report on the shortwave. But neither of us expected much: We were far enough from land by this time that we seldom picked up anything during the day; at night, reception was better, and we could often pull in stations from far off, exotic places.

When Jack emerged a half hour later, he reported the few words he'd been able to make out. "Storm . . . small craft warnings . . . tropical depression . . . Yankees three, Sox two."

"Isn't it awfully early in the year for a tropical depression?" I asked. "Hurricane season isn't supposed to begin for another two *months*."

"I guess we shoulda got that in writing," Jack said with a smile.

While there was still light, we did what we could to get ready. We got out our foul-weather gear. We readied life jackets, harnesses, safety lines, and flashlights. We stowed items we *wouldn't* need, and lashed down everything we could. We ran a radar reflector up the mast to maximize the chance of being spotted on some larger vessel's scope. We checked and double-checked our lines, our pumping system, and our inflatable. We set aside food and drinking water, as well as a change of clothes.

By evening, the entire sky was clouded over, and the seas had flattened. What wind there was still came over our stern, but it was no longer enough to fill our sails, which luffed and sagged. Lines went slack and slapped against the mast, and the boom swung back and forth lazily. We continued to move forward, but our progress seemed due to nothing more than momentum. Our speed dropped to under two knots; we could have walked faster.

With dark, a light rain began to fall, and the air temperature dropped suddenly, so that we were happy to have the warmth of our foul-weather gear. Within an hour, we found ourselves totally becalmed. It was a truly eerie sensation: With neither moon nor stars visible, we were in pitch-blackness, sitting dead still in the middle of the ocean.

We furled the mainsail altogether and tightened down the boom. We shortened the jib and allowed it to hang free at the bow, a once-proud headsail consigned now to the role of a mere telltale. And the tale it told was that there was no wind at all.

I took the wheel while Jack went below to get some rest. But "taking the wheel" proved to be nothing more than a symbolic gesture of assuming command: Without wind, a sailboat simply cannot be steered. I soon gave up trying, I locked the rudder into place and allowed us to drift aimlessly.

An hour went by, and a second one. I dared to think that this would be the extent of our storm: A steady rain - by now somewhere in the moderate to heavy range, but certainly no downpour - and a total absence of wind. I can handle this," I remember telling myself.

Some angry god must have been listening.

A sailor becalmed during daylight hours searches for ripples on the surface of the water - the first signal of a freshening breeze. At night, you have only your sails to watch for signs of life. And after an hour of peering through the darkness, your eyes start playing tricks on you, and you begin to imagine movement when there is none, until you reach the point where you can no longer trust what you see.

So you learn to *feel*.

But even in feeling, I was fooled. I kept expecting that if the breeze was ever going to reappear, it would be at our backs, as before - as indeed it had been for weeks. So when I felt the first breaths upon my *face*, I mistook them for - for what, I don't know. It simply hadn't occurred to me that the wind would do a 180-degree turn. But turn on us it did, and with a vengeance.

It had taken a full day for the wind to die down. It had dropped imperceptibly, in increments too subtle to be noticed. The calm that had followed had been so total that I'd come to believe we'd be in the doldrums forever. But this new wind, coming out of the east and blowing directly into my face, seemed to build in no time. One moment, I was checking the jib to see if indeed it was beginning to pick up the breeze; the next, I was grabbing for the wheel, unlocking the rudder, and winching in the starboard sheet.

A boat under sail can head in any direction you ask her to - almost. The "almost" is reserved for that quarter of the compass that comprises the exact source of the wind itself and the forty degrees or so to either side. Put another way, you can't sail upwind.

But you can come surprisingly close. A boat with a deep keel such as that on *Sea Legs* can make good headway by zigzagging toward the source of the wind, rather than sailing directly into it. The zigs and the zags are called "tacks" (hence, "try a different tack"), and the technique itself is known as "tacking."

Now, by pulling the jib in tight, I tried to head as close to the wind as I could. But I soon found that, without the mainsail, the boat simply wasn't up to the task. So I decided to take a chance and unfurl the main. The difference was immediate and dramatic: Now *Sea Legs* pointed smartly upwind and surged forward eagerly.

A boat beating to the wind, or "close hauled," as we were, leans away from the side the wind is on, or, in nautical terms, "heels to leeward." So steeply did we begin heeling that I had to ease the sails out a bit and steer us off the wind. These adjustments only served to increase our speed, however, and we were soon doing a full ten knots while still heeling sharply. With the wind continuing to build, I knew I'd have to reduce canvas pretty soon, but for the moment I was enjoying the thrill of sailing near the edge.

"Who turned the afterburners on?"

The voice was Jack's, coming from the companionway. His hair was rumpled, and his face creased. The same wind that had roused me from inaction had obviously roused him from sleep.

"I thought it was about time I showed you what this boat can do," I boasted.

"What this boat can do is snap its mast in two," Jack said. "After that, it can't do too much of anything."

He was right, of course. A deep-keeled boat such as *Sea Legs* is almost impossible to knock down. As the force of the wind builds on the sails, the angle of the heel increases, lowering the sails closer to the water on the leeward side. At the same time, the keel rises on the opposite, or windward, side. Think of the keel as a continuation of the mast: Together they form a long lever, not unlike a seesaw. Before that critical point is reached where the sails are forced all the way down to the water and the boat capsizes, the mast will break from the strain. This is a safety feature of sorts, but as safety features go, it's dangerous when activated, as well as expensive and rather humiliating. Not to mention the fact that a boat without a mast is seriously disabled. Demasting is the major threat to transoceanic racers, those heavy-keeled boats that carry oversized and reinforced sails designed to withstand tremendous forces.

Jack disappeared below again, leaving me to wrestle with the wheel and the sheets. When he climbed back up again a few minutes later, he was back in his foul-weather gear. Only now he'd added a life jacket and a safety harness, and he'd brought mine, as well. I put them on while he took the wheel.

By moving our own body weight to the windward side, we were able to balance the boat a bit and continue sailing under full canvas. The wind was still building; it was now so strong that the rigging emitted a low whistling sound. The waves were big enough so that they were breaking all around us, creating whitecaps and slamming hard against our hull. We closed off the companionway to keep the water from getting below, but even in our slicks, we were getting absolutely drenched. The rain seemed to be coming into our faces almost vertically, making it all but impossible to see. And yet I felt nothing but elation. With Jack beside me, I let myself defer to his judgment; I trusted his superior knowledge of the limits of his boat. I knew we could keep going like this for only so long before he'd surrender to caution and give the order to reduce the sails. But in the meantime, we held on, laughing hysterically and shouting to each other in order to be heard over the noise.

"We're sure getting our money's worth!" I yelled. I pointed at the speed indicator. The needle danced between twelve and fourteen knots.

"She's some boat!" Jack shouted.

"You put a lot of work into her!"

I could see him nod.

"And a lot of love!"

"We both did!" he yelled. And it was true: all those hours working on her through the dead of winter, all those freezing shakedown runs of early spring, all those nights I crawled into bed with my bones aching so badly that I couldn't fall asleep. This moment was precisely what we'd been preparing her for, readying her to fly into the teeth of wind and rain just like this. And now she was giving it all back to us.

From nowhere, Jack produced a split of champagne and launched the cork into the weather.

"To the best little lady on the seas!" he toasted. He took a slug from the bottle and handed it to me.

I raised it high. "To my brother the captain!" I shouted, and held the bottle to my lips. The champagne was icy cold, colder by far than the rain. Jack took it back from me.

"To love," he countered, taking another pull.

There was only a mouthful left when he passed it back to me I raised it one last time before draining it.

"To life," I said.

Our euphoria was short-lived. In less than an hour's time, the wind grew to gale force. The rain drove into our faces so hard now, it felt like hailstones. In the darkness, we could barely see the waves, but we estimated them at six to eight feet, and the biggest ones were breaking across our bow. Several times, as we planed forward down the back of a swell, our speed indicator neared twenty knots. We knew we were flirting with the absolute physical limits of our boat.

Jack gave the order to reduce the sails, and we furled both the main and jib to half of their previous size. Even then, we continued to heel and were making eight to ten knots.

"Better tie onto this," Jack shouted, handing me a line. I fastened it to a carabiner on my safety harness while he secured the other end to a stern cleat. Then he repeated the process, tying a second line to himself. Should either of us get knocked over, at least now, we'd have a fighting chance to stay with the boat and get back on board.

Suddenly, there was a flash of white lightning, and the world around us lit up. For a long instant, we could see the waves, see the crests breaking, see how steeply we were riding up one swell and down the next. If the darkness had been frightening because of what we couldn't see, the light was positively terrifying because of what we *could*.

"We're going to have to douse the main altogether!" Jack called, and I fought my way to the furling gear to do it. We'd rigged *Sea Legs* so that all her lines could be handled from the cockpit, and I was grateful for that. Still, moving about within the cockpit itself was nearly impossible. So violently was the boat pitching and yawing and so slippery was the cockpit floor that I dared not take a step without first having two solid handholds. Even then, my feet would slide out from under me in the dark, and I'd bang a knee or gash a shin on some invisible piece of equipment.

It took me some time, but I finally got the mainsail completely furled, so that we were now down to half a jib. But even that proved too much, and while I took the wheel, Jack worked the furling gear until all we were flying was a storm jib, a tiny triangle of headsail.

Though I might get an argument from some stubborn member of the powerboat set, a sailboat in rough seas is inherently more stable than a motor cruiser. Her weighted keel keeps her upright, and her sleek shape offers a minimum of resistance to the oncoming waves, so long as she continues to point into the weather. The storm jib is flown in order to give the helmsman just enough canvas to control the attitude of his craft, the angle he positions her against the sea.

Jack took the wheel now, and I watched as he aimed our bow just a shade off the advancing waves. The trick was to avoid getting broadsided at all costs, allowing a wave to smack into the length of our hull at right angles and wash over us, or - worse still - break us apart. But we also had to guard against getting turned around completely and taking a wave over the stern, for that might flood our cockpit and momentarily disable us, setting us up for a second wave that could capsize us.

We abandoned all notions of making headway. Our only goal became that of riding out the storm. We watched the compass intently, not because we cared where we were going, but because we needed to know in what direction we were *pointing.* I was relieved of my duties as navigator, and I gave up any concern about where we might be on the chart. With no sun or stars to fix on, dead reckoning was out of the question. If we survived - and for me, it was rapidly turning into a matter of *if* - I could always reestablish our position. In the meantime, it had come down to survival, pure and simple.

Nothing in my life had prepared me for the terror I experienced that night. The seas continued to build until we were in waves that reached twenty-five feet. *Sea Legs* bobbed up and down like a cork. We'd ride straight up, as though launched like a surface-to-air missile, then hover momentarily on the crest of some unseen wave before diving back down toward the center of the earth. Huge swells washed over our entire length, and we'd find ourselves completely underwater, fighting for air, clinging desperately to some handrail in the cockpit, or to each other. All this in total darkness; all this in the teeth of driving, unrelenting rain; all this repeating itself over and over and over again.

Jack found a large metal bucket and fastened a line to it. We tied it to the stern and towed it as a jury-rigged sea anchor, hoping to slow the speed of our downward plunges and keep our bow up, lest we "pitchpole" by burying our nose into a trough and be thrown stern over bow.

We took turns at the wheel, fighting to keep the boat pointed upwind. This became so difficult that, at one point, Jack fired up the diesel, figuring we could use its power to help aim us into the wind. But so violently were we being tossed up and down by then that there were moments when our propeller would be lifted completely out of the water, resulting in a whining noise so loud that we feared the increased speed might burn out the bearings of the engine, and so we shut it down.

The rain had soaked through our foul weather gear, and the

wind kept us shivering, but we were too frightened to go below and leave the other alone on deck. I began to think about how absolutely enormous the ocean around us was, how it stretched on for hundreds and thousands of miles in every direction - including beneath us - and how we were nothing but this absurdly tiny speck upon its surface. People cross the Atlantic in ocean liners, in million-ton ships that stretch for blocks. How could we have even *dreamed* that we could do it in a thirty-six-foot piece of fiberglass? Now, I told myself, we were getting exactly what we deserved.

I imagined us getting broadsided, getting swamped, getting knocked over, getting turned upside down. I visualized us driving straight down to the ocean floor and being smashed apart into splinters. In my mind's eye, I saw our mast snap off a hundred times and our boom break loose and pierce our deck and hull. I pictured our electrical system flooding and failing, knocking out our compass light and automatic pumping system, or - worse yet - shorting and bursting into flames. I expected that at any moment we'd be struck by a huge tanker bearing down on us out of the dark, or that we'd ram into some invisible cargo container dislodged from a freighter and floating dead ahead of us. I had the constant sensation that we were taking on huge amounts of water. I was totally convinced that each wave, each plunge from crest to trough, would surely be our last.

I lost all sense of time. It seemed as if hours had gone by - even days, weeks - but when I would look at my watch, I'd see that only ten minutes had passed since last I'd checked The feeling of utter exhaustion that came over me was so intense, so enormous, that I swear there were times I didn't care if I lived or died. That night, I learned to understand suicide; I came to know what it's like to be so worn out, so depleted of reserves, that you feel you can't possibly struggle another minute. You finally reach the point where it takes too much energy to fight the fight, and you realize you've got nothing left to fight it with. You end up not caring anymore; you let go.

Only each time I reached that point, Jack would somehow sense my despair; each time he would press his face up against mine and shout at me over the noise, across the darkness, through the rain, and into the web of numbness that kept closing in around me.

"I think we may be heading for some weather!" he'd yell, or "This can't last more than another two weeks!" And the very sound of his voice would bring me back, would warm me a degree or two, would let me dare to believe we might get through it all.

"Can she really handle this?" I asked him at one point, when it seemed the pounding we were taking was just too much for the boat.

"This and more!" he shouted.

"How about us?" I asked. "Can *we?*"

"Fuckin' aye!" He laughed, turning a sixties' expletive into a nautical rallying cry. And I laughed with him - in spite of my exhaustion, in spite of my fear, in spite of my shivering. I laughed with him.

There's no doubt in my mind that my brother saved my life that night, many times over. I'd thought I was the strong one, but I was wrong. The storm beat me. Not with its intensity, nor its ferociousness, though it had plenty of both. No, it beat me finally with its relentlessness. It outlasted me; it wore me out; it took me to the point where I truly believed it would never end. And even then, even at that moment, there was my kid brother, grabbing me by the shoulders, shaking me back to the business at hand, telling me how great we were doing. Jack fought like a *tiger* that night. He dug his claws into life with a strength and determination I'd never seen before. There was simply nothing on earth that was going to make him lose his grip.

I remember my father once teaching Jack and me how to count the seconds between the flash of lightning and the rumble of thunder to determine how far away the lightning was striking. "One one thousand, two one thousand, three one thousand . . ." I'd count, though to this day, I don't understand just how the thousands are supposed to translate into units of distance. But the best part of it, my father had explained, was that if you saw the lightning *at all*, you knew you were safe: It meant that no matter how quickly the thunder might follow, *you'd already lived through it.*

I was at the wheel. I can no longer remember where Jack was. He might have been next to me, or he might have been somewhere else on deck, checking some piece of equipment or tying down some line slapping in the wind. I was wearing gloves to get a better grip on the smooth surface of the metal. They were leather, and they were soaked through, but they were better than bare hands. I can remember them because they probably saved my life.

It happened all at once. There was a *crack* so loud, so sudden, so *explosive,* I thought my eardrums had been blown out. The entire world turned blindingly white, and a white-hot fireball traveled the length of the mast from top to bottom, where it broke apart and spread out on deck like glowing mercury. I felt an excruciating electric shock run from my fingers through my bowels and out my toes. My mind shrieked at me to let go of the wheel, but I could not, so tightly were my hands frozen to it.

I *know* my heart stopped beating. What I don't understand is what made it start again. The next thing I remember is seeing Jack's face in from of mine, his mouth forming words, but no sounds coming out. I would be stone deaf for the rest of the night. It wouldn't be until the light of morning that I'd discover the flesh of my palms burned through my gloves and the hair on my head singed.

But our father had been right: Even at ground zero, even at the crosshairs of the scope, we'd seen the lightning, which meant we'd lived through it. Though I never want to come that close again, thank you.

The moment had a curious effect on me. With our boat surviving the direct hit of a lightning bolt, I reached a place *beyond terror,* a place where I came to feel that if *that* hadn't finished us off, nothing else would. After that, the horrors of the night receded just a bit for me. The monster waves became hills we were capable of riding up and down; the winds no longer threatened to tear us apart at the seams; the rain was only so much water hurled at our faces. Even the lightning flashing silently around us - I could no longer hear the thunder - seemed less than lethal. We'd taken nature's very worst and somehow come through on the other side. It wasn't that we were *invincible,* the three of us; it was more that we'd already managed to pass the ultimate test, and now whatever lay ahead had simply lost some of its power to terrorize us.

All through the night, we held on together in the cockpit. We took turns at the wheel, took turns staring at the tiny light of the compass, took turns closing our eyes. We did not sleep; we did not eat. When our throats grew dry, we opened our mouths and drank in the rainwater. When our bladders filled, we relieved ourselves right there on deck, and the next wave over the side provided an obliging flush.

With my inability to hear, and the impossibility of seeing in the darkness, our communication was limited to the language of touch. We tapped each other; we hugged; we wrapped an arm around a shoulder; we delivered a reassuring slap on the back or a playful punch to the biceps. And as strange as it is to tell, we even held hands for long stretches of time, we two macho sons of the homophobic fifties. And together, we made it through the night, my brother and I.

* * *

Morning brought no sunrise, only a gradual awareness that we could see beyond the rail of our boat. We still rose and fell on fifteen-foot waves. The rain continued, but in the light, it seemed not quite so hard as before, and not quite so vertical in its onslaught.

The wind had shifted, so now it came out of the southwest. Perhaps it was that shift, or perhaps it was the change from night to day - or maybe it was nothing but our imaginations - but it seemed not so cold as it had felt in the darkness.

My deafness gave way to a steady ringing noise in my ears, and eventually I could distinguish individual sounds, but it would be some time before my hearing returned to anything approaching normal.

With the light, we were able to inspect *Sea Legs* for damage. A section of our railing had been badly bent and we'd taken a tear in our jib and lost a buoy or two overboard; besides that, everything had survived intact. We ventured below, where - despite our efforts in lashing things down and sealing the cabin closed - a fair amount of equipment had found its way to the floor and taken a good soaking. But we'd sustained no real damage to speak of, a testament to the seaworthiness of our boat, or to dumb luck, or maybe a bit of both.

I fired up the stove, which was ingeniously suspended on gimbals designed to keep it level regardless of the boat's motion. While the principle may have been sound, the practice lagged somewhat behind, and it proved to be tricky business. I made coffee, dark and strong and hot, which we half-slurped and half-spilled in the cockpit, burning our tongues and laughing at our clumsiness.

* * *

By noon, both the wind and the rain had fallen off appreciably, and the seas were down to ten feet. We laughed at the waves, we mocked the whitecaps. I found myself thinking in military terms, noticing, for example, that it no longer seemed as though we were the storm's target of choice. For I truly felt as though I'd come through a *war*. I imagined how a soldier must feel after living through the worst of a nightmarish battle, no longer startled by the muffled thud of an occasional shell exploding off in some distant field.

The clouds began breaking up towards nightfall, and the seas continued to flatten. The rain still fell, but only intermittently, and with no driving fury behind it.

We began the transition back to normalcy: We replaced the jib and set our sails once again, we retrieved our storm anchor, we untied our safety lines and took off our life vests and harnesses, we even changed into dry clothes.

That night, we placed our trust in the self-steering device. We went below, cooked, and ate for the first time in a day and a half. We broke open a good bottle of red wine, and I filled two glasses.

"To life!" I toasted, as I had at the beginning of the storm.

I could see from Jack's expression that he wanted to correct me, but I was still too deaf to hear his voice. Nonetheless, by reading his lips, I was able to make out his words.

"To *living*" is what he said.

7

All my life, I've been a great believer in omens, in signs from the heavens. Spotting a rainbow is a sure promise of good things to come. Finding a coin and picking it up can bring good luck, but only if it's head's-up; if it's tails, better to leave it where it is.

So when I awoke the next morning to sunlight slanting into the cabin, my first reaction was nothing less than a feeling that I'd been reborn. I lay on my bunk, squinting into the light, listening to the sounds of *Sea Legs* under sail. There was the whooshing of the sea as it parted for our bow, the slapping of the wind against our sails, the groaning of the hull. At one point, I made out the ratcheting of a winch being grinded. It struck me that the combination of sounds was not unlike a symphony, a coming together of different parts, different instruments, different voices. I must have listened for a good ten minutes before it suddenly dawned on me: *I could hear again!*

I climbed up on deck, expecting to find Jack at the wheel. And I did, sort of. He was sprawled out on the bench, his head propped up against a flotation cushion, his hat pulled down over his eyes. His feet were bare, one dangled beneath him, the other rested on the wheel, apparently in charge of the steering. His hands were occupied nestling an open can of beer.

"What time is it?" I asked, staring at the beer. Neither of us had ever been much of a drinker, even at more traditional times of day.

"Oh, this?" Jack looked at his beer and laughed. "I've always wanted to try one for breakfast," he said. "I figured now's as good a time as any."

"And?"

He answered with a long, full-bodied belch, the sort we used to summon as kids when we were engaged in contests to see who could be more disgusting. At one point in our teens, we'd devised an elaborate rating system, all the way from a one (assigned to the politest of mini-burps) to a ten (reserved for an all-out, window-rattling moose belch). We'd even mastered the art of belch-talking, explaining to our mother that you could never tell - it might come in handy if one of us ever had to undergo a laryngectomy. But this time, I let Jack's opening salvo go unanswered. I was afraid that if I tried to top it so early in the morning, I might end up losing the previous night's dinner, which would be grounds for automatic disqualification.

"We've got company," Jack said, extending his beer can as a pointer.

And he was right: An escort of dolphins was spread out on either side of our bow. There must have been two dozen of them, perfectly attuned to our speed, gliding effortlessly from wave to wave. We hadn't seen dolphins since the very first hint of bad weather. Like Jack, they'd sensed the sea change early. Now they were back.

Sunlight, blue sky, and the return of the dolphins! How could I not feel my spirits soaring? How could I have asked for a more fitting moment to shrug off the cloak of ignorance and confront the mystery that Jack had created?

"So," I said, trying my best to sound matter-of-fact. "What's the story with Walker Island?"

"I told you," Jack answered. "There is no Walker Island."

"So you did. But you never bothered to tell me where we *are* going, if there's no Walker Island."

"You never asked." As though I needed him to remind me of my days spent in avoidance.

"That was then," I said.

"And now?"

"Now I'm asking."

"Are you sure?" He took a long swig of his beer.

"I'm sure," I said, though the truth is, I'd never been less sure of anything in my life. But by bringing the matter up, I sensed that I'd passed some point of no return. Having once asked where it was that we were going, I now had no choice but to press on for an answer.

And I got one.

"We're going to where Walker Island would be," Jack said, "if there *were* a Walker Island." He said this as though everything were quite self-evident, and it was I who was somehow missing the obvious.

"Sorry," I said. "I still don't get it." But I was beginning to, and by now I think we both knew it.

All this time, Jack had been studying the sails, alert for

any subtle shift in the wind that might require a steering correction. Now he allowed his gaze to wander to the horizon.

"We're still going to the same spot," he said. "Thirty-one north latitude, sixty-five west longitude, give or take a few miles. Same as before."

"What's there?" I asked, the dread building, the blood beginning to pound in my ears.

"Oh, about 10,000 feet of water," Jack said calmly. He continued to look off to where sea met sky,

"That's all?"

"That's all."

"And what happens there?" I asked, though by now I surely knew. Still, I guess I needed to hear it from him.

For the first time, Jack met my gaze with his. "That's where I get off," he said softly. "That's where this trip ends for me."

If I could free some sleeping genie from an old lamp or dusty bottle and be granted but a single wish, it would surely be to travel back through time to those days aboard *Sea Legs* before I made my brother tell me what was to happen once we'd reached our phantom destination. And if the genie trifled with me and told me that the best he could do would be to transport me back one tick of time, to the very instant before I demanded Jack's actual explanation, then I'd settle for that. I'd willingly go back to the *dread* if only I could avoid the *knowing*. And to those who would disagree and insist that's it's always better to know, I would say this: No, not always.

Because *The Log of the Sea Legs* contains no entries for a full three days following that terrible notation - "Today Jack told me about Walker Island" - I have no written record of the period. During the storm itself, I was too occupied with the business of survival to write; afterward I was too distraught by Jack's words to put them on paper. But my memory is raw enough to enable me to re-create our conversation with the same degree of certainty with which you might recite what you ate for breakfast this morning. Some recollections owe their vividness to recentness, others to a long-term lender far greedier in what he takes as interest.

"When we get to 'Walker Island,'" Jack explained now, "I'm going to say good-bye to you. We're going to hug. We're both going to cry some. Then I'm going to walk to the bow of the boat. From there, I'm going to dive into the ocean."

"And me?"

"You? You're going to turn the boat around and take her home."

"Just like that?" I asked.

"Just like that."

My first reaction was one of pure denial, insistence that Jack was joking. "You can't be serious!" I said, doing my best to keep the terror from cracking my voice and betraying me. "You've got to be kidding!"

"Sorry," Jack said. "But I'm afraid I'm not kidding."

Still, Denial can be a seductive mistress, who tends to cling long after the affair has ended. I absolutely refused to hear what Jack was telling me.

"I don't believe this!" I shouted. "You can't be serious!"

"I'm dead serious," Jack assured me. "If you'll pardon the pun."

"I won't pardon anything! And I won't accept what you're telling me, Is this your idea of some stupid April Fools' joke?"

"We're well into May," Jack reminded me.

Surely there came a point where even I could hear my protestations begin to ring false. Each time Jack told me how serious he was, I'd voice my disbelief all over again. But inside, I must have known full well that, April or May, this was anything but a joke.

For as I began to think back, the pieces started to fall into place, bit by bit. Why, after all, had Jack gone to such trouble to rig *Sea Legs* so that all her lines could be managed single-handed, when there were two of us? Why had he bothered to install furling gear for the mainsail, or add the self-steering device? Why had he been so insistent that I become proficient with the sextant and be the one to master the art of dead reckoning? There was but a single answer to all of these questions, I realized now: Jack had known from the outset that he wouldn't be coming back. He'd brought me along - among other reasons, perhaps - so that there'd be somebody on board to turn the boat around and sail her back when the time came.

It strikes me now that in continuing to insist that my brother was joking while these facts stared me in the face, I was playing the first of a series of cards from my hand: Even as Jack assured me that he was completely serious, I was deliberately treating his idea as absurd, as nothing short of totally ludicrous. By holding it up to ridicule, I was hoping that I might somehow manage to belittle it, to reduce it to something comical and bizarre - and thus force him to rethink the whole business.

I went to bed at the end of that day still refusing to acknowledge that my only brother really intended to throw himself into the ocean. I was determined to spend one more night wrapped in the comforting arms of Denial. But it was a fitful sleep, of grudging minutes far apart; when finally I awoke bleary-eyed in the morning, my mistress had vanished from my side for good.

8

Morning brought more than the loss of denial. It brought clear skies and a fresh breeze from the south. It also brought anger.

I can even recall the instant it arrived. One moment, Jack and I were sipping coffee in the cockpit, talking about the change in the wind.

"Another storm?" I asked him.

"No, I don't think so," he said. "The prevailing wind changes around this time of year. It'll make things easier on you bringing her back."

It caught me like a punch in the nose, all over again. I held my tongue for a moment, but the anger was there, and I couldn't contain it.

"So tell me," I said, "when did you make this little decision of yours?" I don't know just *what* I thought his answer might be. I guess I half-expected him to say, "Last month," or "A few days ago." I probably wouldn't have been too surprised if he'd said, "Yesterday."

He squinted for a moment, as though trying to remember."Almost a year ago," he said. "I started thinking about it the day I found out I was sick. I had some more tests to see if there might be some mistake. There wasn't. So I went to the library, did some reading on prognosis, onset of symptoms, treatment. It didn't take me too long to decide I didn't need any part of it. At that point, I sat down and asked myself what I wanted to do with the rest of my life, while I was still well enough to do it."

"But that's just it!" I shouted. "You *are* still well! You could be well for another *year.* You could live another five, maybe another *ten* years!"

Jack shook his head. "I don't want those years," he said calmly. *"This* is what I wanted." And to demonstrate, he swept his hand across the deck, across the horizon beyond it. "And," he added, "I wanted it with you."

I should have felt honored, I suppose. I should have felt trusted, rewarded, deeply loved.

I felt nothing but rage.

"So you *lied* to me, you bastard! You tricked me aboard!"

Jack nodded. "It was the only way I could pull it off." He smiled. "I was afraid you wouldn't come otherwise."

"You're damn right I wouldn't have come!"

"See?"

"And I wouldn't have let *you* go, either."

"Yes, you would have," Jack said. "And after we'd fought about it for a week or so, you would've come along, too. But fighting onshore would've been much nastier - you trying to keep me from going, bringing all sorts of other people into it."

"No one else knows?"

"No one else knows."

"You haven't bothered to mention to your daughters the little fact that you won't be coming back from this trip?" I was incredulous.

"No," Jack admitted. "And that was hard. But I don't think they could've handled it quite like that. This way, they'll be okay. They'll always be able to think I died doing what I loved most in life."

"What you love most in life is killing yourself?"

"No." Jack smiled. "You're going to tell them I was washed over in the storm."

"I'm supposed to *lie* for you?"

"Some lies are good lies. 'Fibs,' we call them."

The rage within me built with every exchange. It was dawning on me that Jack had thought of everything; he'd mapped out each step of his plan with meticulous detail. He now unfolded it all for me in absolute calm. And I think it was that very calmness that infuriated me most.

"Have you told your wife?" I asked him.

"Ex-wife," he corrected me.

"Ex-wife."

"No. But she's a smart woman I suspect she pretty much knows."

I remembered her words to me at the send-off party, as she'd pulled me aside on the dock and looked me hard in the eye. "She made me promise to bring you back safely."

"You see?"

"And *me,* you bastard. What about *me?*"

"You'll be all right," Jack said. "If you're worried about sailing her back alone, head up to Bermuda first, take on a mate. Take on a whole *crew* if you like."

"*Goddamn* you!" I screamed, going for his neck. We hadn't fought since we were kids, trading blows with plastic toys, or books, or whatever else happened to be handy and not too lethal. "I'm not talking about some fucking *boat!*" I shouted, my arms flailing wildly, tears streaming down my face. "I'm talking about me, Jack. I'm your brother."

He caught me in his arms and held me close.

"Who's going to lie to *me?*" I sobbed. "Who's going to lie to *me?*"

Fifteen years later, I have difficulty piecing the rest of the day together. I can remember crying; I can remember arguing; I can remember beating my fists against my brother's chest at one point in a child's tantrum, though I can no longer recall the exact remark or comment that set me off. And all the while, Jack maintained his infuriating calm. In time, he'd explained that it was only his way of trying to project a sense of certainty, of letting me know that he'd thought everything out long ago and made up his mind once and for all. He'd wanted me to realize that there was nothing I could do about it. That way, I wouldn't feel responsible for his decision, and in time I'd be able to accept it.

"Never," I'd promised him. "Never."

Anger has a certain energizing quality to it, and rage can sustain us for a while. But the human body can pump just so much adrenaline before exhaustion eventually takes over. By early afternoon, I felt totally drained, almost unable to keep my head up. I went below to find escape in my bunk.

I must have been slept out by then, however, because I found myself lying awake, staring at the ceiling above my head, feeling the motion of the boat beneath me. My thoughts drifted back to the storm, to how it had tested us, and how each of us had met that test.

Unlike Jack, I'd come aboard *Sea Legs* without any ambiguity about living: I'd brought with me no desire whatsoever to die. But as things had turned out, in the middle of the night, when I'd succumbed to believing that the storm would go on forever until it would kill us, I'd been ready to die, to give it all up. But Jack - Jack, who already knew that in ten days' time he'd be throwing himself over the rail; Jack, who so easily could have surrendered to the sea and let it take him right then and there - Jack had put me to shame with what I could only explain as a fierce determination to survive, a *will to live*. In my darkest hour, I'd had Jack to keep me going. What had Jack had? What reserves had he been able to draw on, at a time when I was so absorbed in my own fear, and so overwhelmed by my own exhaustion, as to be totally useless to him?

I chose to overlook the possibility that Jack's fight had been for *my* life, I preferred to believe it had been for his own. And if I was right, didn't that mean that Jack wanted to live in spite of everything he was telling me? Wasn't it painfully obvious that he was crying out for me to tell him how deeply he was loved, how desperately he was needed? Wasn't it plain to see that, at the moment of truth, he'd chosen life after all? I seized on that notion the way a man overboard grabs at a log when he'll have only one chance at it; I clung to it as though I were clinging to hope itself.

My brother had saved my life. Now it was my turn to save his.

With a renewed sense of resolve, I climbed from my bunk and made my way up the companionway. No missionary ever went forth to preach conversion with greater love in his heart or more righteousness in his soul.

I found the target of my ministries at the wheel, studying the reflection of his face in a small pocket mirror. He was wearing an old pair of cutoffs, a red baseball cap, and aviator sunglasses - nothing more. I was struck again by how tan and fit he looked. At thirty-nine, there wasn't a visible ounce of fat on Jack. His hair had thinned a bit and had begun turning gray here and there; otherwise, he could have passed for ten years younger.

Catching sight of me, Jack palmed the mirror and pocketed it, apparently embarrassed at being caught in his little act of vanity.

"That was a quick nap," he observed.

"I missed you."

Jack smiled. "Should I say, 'That's nice,'" he asked, "or should I get ready for a speech?"

"Get ready for anything you like," I said. "If you think I'm going to be a good sport about all this, you're out of your mind."

To Jack's credit, he had the decency to say nothing.

"You saved my life," I told him "You were magnificent during the storm; you were *awesome.* Here I was, ready to quit. Damn it, I *would have quit* if it hadn't been for you."

"Nonsense," he said. "If I'd been the one who was having trouble, somehow you'd have found the strength to be there for me."

"Maybe, maybe not. But don't you see? Now you *are* the one having trouble. Let *me* be the one to be here for you on this.

Let me take you back home and care for you. Let me help you through this, okay?

"Jack looked straight at me without speaking. And as I studied his face, his features seemed to relax before my eyes. He let his forehead unfurrow just a bit; the lines around his eyes softened visibly; even his mouth and jaw unclenched. All of the toughness seemed to melt away, replaced by a gentleness that had been absent during our recent exchanges, a gentleness that had always been such an important part of the Jack I knew.

"Do you really want to help me?" he asked softly. Gone was the glibness from his tone, gone the casualness that I'd been finding so infuriating ever since Jack had revealed his plan to me.

I let his words sink in, afraid I might spoil things by jumping too quickly to answer him. To this day, I can remember the long moment of silence, filled only by the sensation of my pulse beating in my temples, as I dared to hope that I'd finally broken through some invisible barrier and reached him.

"Of course I want to help you," I said at last, matching the softness of Jack's voice with my own.

"Then please let me do what I've got to do."

Spoken every bit as softly, every bit as gently as his earlier words. But making it absolutely clear that his resolve was as strong as ever. So much for hope, I told myself.

"I don't get it," I said. "I don't understand how you can possibly want to go through with this. Here you are, on top of the world, at the absolute peak of your strength, physically and mentally. You don't even have symptoms. Yet you're ready to throw in the towel."

"That's just the point," Jack said. "I was only able to do what I did during the storm because I'm still well. Six months from now, a year from now, I'd have been too sick, too weak. I don't ever want to be in that position."

"But why the rush?" I demanded. "Why *now?*"

"I think that's the wrong question," Jack said. "Why is it such a sin to want to quit when I'm ahead, to want to go out while I'm on top?"

"You make it sound like you're at a casino," I said, "like life is nothing more than some kind of dice game."

"It is, in a way. And the trouble with most players is, they're never satisfied with winning. They've always got to try one more roll of the dice. They can't quit until they've begun to give some of their winnings back to the house. Then, as they walk away, all they can think of is how they should've quit while they were ahead."

"But you've got time," I insisted. "You've got real quality time left. Why not wait and see, for God's sake?"

Jack reached out and put a hand on my upper arm. "I don't want to get to that point," he said. "You're absolutely right when you say I'm on top of the world. And that's precisely where I want to end up. I refuse to give anything back to the house. I'm going to be the one who walks away from the table a winner."

"Why can't you at least wait until the symptoms begin?" I argued. "What is it you're so afraid of?"

Jack was silent for a moment. Good, I thought, he doesn't have all the answers, after all. But his silence was a brief one.

"The symptoms have already begun," he said. "That mirror you caught me looking at before? It isn't about vanity: It's not supposed to tell me I'm the fairest in the land. It's supposed to tell me how much my gums are bleeding today. Jesus, Joe, do you know what it's like, waking up each morning and finding new spots on your skin, or feeling lumps where there shouldn't be any? Wondering whether the headaches you get or the tremor in your hand mean you've got a tumor the size of a golf ball growing inside your brain?"

"My gums bleed, too," I said. "My dentist tells me it's because I don't take care of them. And everybody gets spots - it's probably just too much sun."

"And the headaches? The tremors?"

"Those may be nothing," I said. "We get back home, I'll go to the doctor with you. We'll have all of these things checked out. They may turn out to be nothing."

"This time."

"Yeah, this time," I agreed. "Hey, Jack, nobody ever promised us *forever,* you know. Lots of people go through stuff like this, and much worse. Help me out here, will you? I just don't understand what it is you're so afraid of."

Jack seemed to consider that for a moment. "I guess what I'm most afraid of is that I'll learn to cope," he said. "It'll go something like this. First, I'll come down with a cough. I'll tell myself, Hey, it's not so bad, I can deal with that. Next, I'll find out it's pneumonia. Okay, I'll take antibiotics; I'll get over it. After that, it'll be headaches. So I'll learn to live with the pain, or I'll take enough pills to get through the days in a fog. I'll say, No problem, I can do this. Before you know it, I'll be signing up for chemotherapy, radiation, bone-marrow transplants, surgery. They'll be poisoning me, burning me, slicing little pieces off me, and there I'll be, thanking them, counting my blessings, grateful to be alive still."

We'd lived through our father's death ten years earlier, and it seemed clear that this was a pointed reference to it. Dad had bought an extra couple of years from his doctors at the end, but they were tough years, full of pain and setbacks, and I'd never known if he'd been glad he'd put himself through it or not. Apparently, Jack had come to his own conclusion about it.

"No one's asking you to go through bone-marrow transplants, Jack."

"Not today they're not. But we let these things sneak up on us; we develop a *tolerance*. They convince you to take the chemotherapy, see how it works. So your hair falls out, big deal. They tell you there are more important things than vanity; if you like, you can always get a wig. Dad got to the point where he let them cut off his *balls,* for Chrissakes. He joked about it afterward. 'Didn't have much use for the damn things at my age, anyway,' he said. Remember that?"

I remembered that.

"Don't you see?" Jack asked me. "Once I let them start with me, I commit to the process; I willingly accept one indignity after another. And for what? For a few months of remission here or there? For a couple of years of pain and procedures? For living some shadow version of my former self, dependent upon doctors and nurses and drugs and - "

"Family."

"Why? Just so I can prolong the inevitable?"

"We're all going to die, Jack. It's not some kind of race, you know."

"But it doesn't have to be some kind of endurance contest, either, where we stay in it long after we should've had the good sense to drop out. Think of all the athletes who weren't smart enough to know when to quit. Think of Joe Louis, getting knocked to the canvas by guys who weren't good enough to lace up his gloves when he was in his prime. Think of Willie

Mays struggling to hit two seventy-three his last season, or Bob Cousy too slow to bring the ball upcourt anymore.

I looked at my brother and, for the first time, I thought I knew his terror. There'd been no sign of it during the storm, when I'd most expected to see it, when I myself was so paralyzed that the life all but went out of me. No, it wasn't death that frightened Jack, I suddenly understood, it wasn't the loss of life that he ultimately feared. It was the loss of control, the loss of *self.*

My insight into Jack's thinking allowed me to let up a bit on him. I don't know now if I was being charitable toward him in my new awareness, or if I was simply taking time to regroup and refine my strategy. Whichever it was, it gave the two of us some breathing room. And it also permitted us to get back just a bit to the business of sailing.

The southern breeze now warmed us and dried us out. We straightened our damaged rail and mended our torn jib. We hung our wet clothing and gear on makeshift lines. I got out my sextant and took shots of the sun, went to my conversion tables and reestablished our position. From it, I was able to reconstruct our course during the storm. We'd been pointed east the whole time, and though we'd been heading into the wind, I'd had the distinct sensation that we'd been moving forward, up one wave and down the next, as the sea rushed by us from bow to stern. Now my calculations told me that we'd actually been pushed *back* almost twenty miles in two days.

I decided to postpone the inevitable issue of our destination; there'd be time to confront it. I charted a course as before, to thirty-one north latitude, sixty-five west longitude, to where Walker Island would have been, had there been a Walker Island.

That afternoon, while I took the wheel, Jack rigged up a fishing line and trolled a lure from the stern. In the space of an hour, he'd landed a baby kingfish, a yellow snapper, and two flying fish. We tossed the king and snapper back, keeping the flying fish and sautéing them for dinner that night. When fresh, there's no better eating fish in the world: The meat is tender, flaky, and sweet, and needs nothing but a little lemon or lime squeezed onto it. But as good as it tasted, I found myself less than hungry, and I pushed most of my portion onto Jack's plate.

Afterward, we sat in the cockpit and watched a quarter-moon rise in a cloudless sky. The breeze had dropped off, and we were doing maybe five knots over two-foot waves. Compared to the storm, it seemed like lake sailing.

"Do you have any idea how much I love you?" I asked Jack.

"Yes," he said softly. "And I also have a pretty good idea of how hard this has got to be for you."

"How about your daughters? They love you, too, you know?"

"I know." He nodded. "But they'll cope. They'll be okay. They've got their mother, and they've got each other. My life insurance will get them through college with something to spare. That'll help."

Here I was talking about love while Jack was thinking of insurance and tuition payments. But I took the bait, so ready I was to confront him on any level he might choose. "Did you ever stop to think that there might be an exclusion for suicide?" I suggested. "That the company might not pay off so quickly?"

"What suicide?" Jack asked. "There was a storm, remember? We didn't make that up. There'll be weather reports to confirm it. I was washed overboard."

"Oh, I get it. First it was a benevolent fib to keep your girls from knowing the truth. Now I'm supposed to be an accomplice to insurance fraud."

"There's no fraud," Jack assured me. "I checked the policy. After a waiting period, it covers suicide. So it doesn't matter what you tell them."

"That's crazy. Anyone could go out and buy a million dollars' worth of coverage, wait till it kicks in, and say good-bye."

"I suppose you're right. That waiting period's the catch, though: It's two years. Seems with most people, the urge to die wears off at some point during that time. But even if it doesn't, the companies have got it all figured out and reduced to numbers. They've got these actuarial tables that show them that if they sell insurance to 10,000 non-smoking, thirty-five year-old white males, precisely fourteen of them are going to kill themselves at some point during the life of their policies. It's all calculated and built into the rates; they don't care. If it turns out they're wrong, and suicide suddenly goes out of style, say, then the state regulators step in, make them reduce their premiums. So it's no difference to them."

"And what if suicides go *up?* Suppose everybody were to decide to cop out and take the easy way out?"

"I don't think that's likely," Jack said.

"Oh no? It happens with teenagers all the time. Some high school kid can't deal with his pimples, takes a dive off a bridge. A week later, his girlfriend decides she can't go on living without him. The papers get a hold of it, write it up like a *Romeo and Juliet* thing. Before you know it, you're reading about copycats all over the county. They call it the 'tipping point,' where you reach a critical mass and all of a sudden you've got a full-blown epidemic on your hands."

"Sorry," Jack said with a wry smile, "but I refuse to be held responsible for an epidemic of suicides."

As much as I wanted to keep up my attack on Jack, I knew I

had to back off at some point and give him breathing room. The last thing I wanted to do was to turn things into a contest of wills, where the focus of our dialogue would shift from who was right and who was wrong to who could dig his heels in deeper and be more stubborn. So as we sat that evening and watched the moon climb higher and higher in the sky, I forced myself to let go for a while. I let the night envelop us with her darkness and her soothing symphony of sounds. I let myself be transported back to those glorious sun-drenched days and magical moonlit nights, when we'd sailed in pure, perfect joy, with nothing but the horizon ahead of us - days and nights that were in truth barely behind us, but which now seemed ages ago, millennia ago. I saw them all in my mind's eye, a movie being rewound in excruciatingly slow motion; back to before my brother had looked me in the eye and revealed his terrible plan to me; back further, to before there'd been a storm and a bolt of lightning that should have killed us both right then and there; all the way back to a time when everything was warm and dry and safe and I still believed there was a place called Walker Island.

9

One of the results of Jack's revelation to me about his plan to kill himself was that I no longer felt I could trust him. Whereas before I'd gone along with his little game of withholding the final charts from me, I now took it upon myself to dig them out and inspect them one afternoon while Jack was busy at the wheel. On doing so, I made a macabre - but not entirely unexpected - discovery: I saw that Jack had actually gone to the trouble of locating thirty-one north latitude, sixty-five west longitude and there, at the precise spot where the lines intersected, he'd inked in a dot and, next to it, had written "Walker Island."

I looked up from the chart and caught Jack watching me, just before he had a chance to avert his eyes. We both knew I'd seen his notation, there seemed no point in pretending otherwise.

"Why that dot," I asked him, "if there's nothing there?"

Jack shrugged. "It's as good a spot as any," he said. "I had to pick *someplace*."

"Suppose I miss it? I *am* the navigator, after all."

Jack seemed to think about it for a moment. "I guess I could settle for some other place," He said. "If I have to."

The thought panicked me. Was he telling me that he might go overboard anywhere, at any time that suited him? Was he now going to deprive me of the small comfort I'd been able to take from knowing that we were still several hundred miles away from our destination and that I therefore still had time to talk him out of going through with his plan? A rush of fear came over me, and my mind raced to find some way to keep those miles and that time as a buffer between us and the dot on the chart. And as I look back now at the bargain I managed to strike in my desperation, I regard it as nothing less than Faustian, my own version of a deal with the Devil.

"I'll keep us headed to 'Walker Island'" is what I told my brother, "if you'll promise me you won't do anything before we get there."

So help me, I spoke those very words, right down to the horrible, cowardly euphemism "do anything." And Jack - Jack said nothing. Instead, he looked me in the eye, and then he nodded once, and we had our bargain. And all I'd had to promise was that I'd deliver my only brother to the place of his death.

But if I now know that I sold my soul that afternoon, at the time, all I felt was relief. I'd fashioned a good deal, after all: I'd bought time, precious time I could use to work on Jack. Back at the charts, I made some hasty calculations and concluded that if conditions held as they were, we still had roughly six days of sailing ahead of us.

I reminded myself that I was a lawyer, a lawyer and a writer. I made my living day in and day out using words to persuade people - clients, witnesses, prosecutors, judges, juries, editors, readers, reviewers. Here I'd been handed a case where logic was clearly on my side, not to mention love, and life itself. And I had to persuade only one person - my own brother, the same baby brother I'd once managed to convince he'd been adopted after being raised by cats.

How could I possibly fail?

"Did it ever occur to you how utterly selfish you're being?" I asked Jack that evening. We were doing the dinner dishes, after another meal of freshly caught fish. Once again, I'd eaten less than Jack. It was turning into something of a pattern: As we drew closer to the tiny dot on the chart, my brother's appetite grew; he seemed to savor every mouthful of food, every sip of drink. I, on the other hand, found myself less and less hungry, and eating - which had long been one of our great shared pleasures on board - began to become something of a chore for me.

"Sure, I'm being selfish," Jack agreed. "But what on earth do I have a right to be selfish about, if not my own life?"

"I'm not talking about a *right* here, Jack. I'm trying to get you to see that what you do affects other people. It has *consequences*."

"No man is an island?"

"Sure," I agreed. "There's some truth to that."

Jack handed me the last of the dishes. I dried it and put it away. We killed the cabin lights, and I followed Jack up the companionway and into the cockpit. It was a good ten degrees cooler on deck, and the breeze felt good. The sky was almost dark, except behind us to the west, where a narrow band of purple still marked the horizon. There were already stars everywhere. I thought about taking a shot of Polaris with the sextant, then decided it could wait. By now, dead reckoning had lost some of its early charm for me.

"I know how this affects you," Jack said. "I know it'll affect my daughters, too, and my ex-wife. I'm sorry for that, I really am. But I don't know what to do about it."

"You can change your mind." I've always believed in the power of understatement.

Jack shook his head slowly. "I don't want to do that," he said. "I've decided what's right for me. I don't want to become sick. I don't want to begin the process of turning into an invalid. I'm sure about that, surer than I've ever been about anything before. Now you're telling me that I should forget what I want, and instead do what'll make other people happy."

"I'll accept that," I said, "if that's what it takes."

"You're asking too much of me."

"For God's sake, all I'm asking is for you to go on living, to refrain from killing yourself!"

"For how long?"

I took Jack's question as his first indication of uncertainty. I knew I had to be careful; I couldn't ask for too much. "I don't know," I said. "How about we just see how it goes?"

"We know how it's going to go, Joe."

"Yeah," I admitted. "But we don't know how soon it's going to start, how quickly it's going to progress, how much quality time you might have left. Why not try to squeeze out whatever good stuff you can?"

To the north, a shooting star made a long arc to the horizon.

"Here's the way I look at it," Jack said. "For almost forty years

I've been surrounded by people who love me, blessed with good health, and lucky enough to do everything I've ever wanted to do. I'm on top of the mountain. I've got nowhere else to go but down. I know exactly what's down there, and I want no part of it. So I've got a choice: I can call it quits right now, at the perfect moment, or I can put it off and spend some time suffering before I get around to doing it. But who wins that way? I certainly don't, and I can't see how you do, or my girls, either. Not in the long run."

"There is no long run," I said. "Life is too short as it is. I want you with me for as much of it as possible."

Jack smiled. *"Now* who's being selfish?" he asked.

"You're damn right I'm being selfish," I snapped. "You're the only brother I've got. What's wrong with my wanting to keep you alive?"

"Nothing," Jack said. "Truth is, I'd be awfully upset if you didn't."

The sky was beginning to lighten to the south, where the moon would soon make its appearance. I searched the heavens for another shooting star, knowing that there was precious little time left to spot one. I felt that if I could see just one more before the moon made it impossible, it would be a good sign.

"I'm not going to be able to deal with your death," I said, "I'm just not going to be able to handle it."

"I'm afraid you're going to have to, one way or another," Jack said. "Wouldn't you rather remember me as healthy, strong, happy? Instead of wasting away in some hospital bed somewhere, with a tube up my nose, an IV in my arm, a catheter in my penis, a bedpan under my butt? Maybe I'll be writhing in pain. Maybe I'll have enough morphine in me that I won't be. If I'm having a good day, we'll be able to talk for a few minutes. But then I might not know your name -

or mine, for that matter. I'll drool. My gums will bleed. My breath will smell so putrid, you'll be afraid to come near my mouth. My back will be raw with bedsores. My skin will be gray and covered with ulcers. I'll need someone else to feed me, to wash me, to shave me, to brush my teeth, to *diaper* me. Why in the name of heaven do you want me to go through that? And why would you want to remember me like that?"

I tried to say, "I'd still love you," but my voice caught in the middle of it.

Jack must have heard me anyway. "I know you would," he said gently. "But don't make me become that for you. Love me enough *now* not to make me go through that."

I couldn't think of an answer to that, and I was afraid my voice would abandon me, so I let it rest. But it was so difficult for the trial lawyer in me to let the other guy get the last word that I had to keep reminding myself there was nobody else around. It was just my brother and me; there was no jury to win over, no audience to impress.

The tip of the moon finally made its appearance off our starboard side. We watched as it cleared the horizon and began its climb. The night was so clear that it seemed as though we could see the dark portion of the moon, but maybe that was only our imaginations straining.

I thought of my wife back ashore, and of my children. I wondered what they were doing this evening, what it was they were watching this very moment, as the same moon that rose in our sky worked its way west, toward theirs. Was it the pages of a homework assignment, or the glossy ads of some magazine? Was it the passing traffic at a nearby mall, or a giant movie screen in an air-conditioned theater, or some rerun of an old TV series? I knew how incredibly lucky I should have been feeling to be able to watch a perfect moon rise over nothing but vast expanses of ocean in every direction; instead, I felt cheated, robbed of any sense of joy that should have been mine. Home seemed half a world away, and I ached with envy of those who'd been smart enough to stay there.

10

There came a point when I began to reckon time in terms of how many days were left until we'd reach the tiny dot inked on the final chart, a countdown to whatever final confrontation lay ahead of my brother and me. I played out various scenarios in my mind. There was the one where I deliberately missed our mark, causing us to sail past the dot and thus avoid the moment of truth. There was the one where I turned us around prematurely while Jack slept, then headed us back for the mainland without ever reaching "Walker Island." There was even one where I overpowered my brother, locked him below, and took him back in chains.

There were also many versions where I succeeded in winning Jack over with the sheer force of my words, countless variations where I managed to come up with the absolutely irrefutable argument, the perfect plea, to which he had no choice but to give in. These versions became more than fantasies: In time, I took the best of them and presented them to Jack. But each absolutely irrefutable argument I served up somehow came out less than fully persuasive, and each perfectly crafted plea I made failed to break Jack's resolve.

Day Four dawned with me already at the wheel. I was sleeping at odd hours by this time, rising early, often collapsing by midafternoon, waking up again in time for dinner, but generally finding myself too tired to have much interest in eating. Later, I'd be unable to fall asleep at night. After a while, I'd give up trying, and by four or five in the morning, I'd be up all over again, on deck, waiting for sunrise. Jack seemed to experience no such difficulty: He'd fallen into a regular pattern and seemed to thrive on it, joining me by six or seven, looking well rested and fit, wanting to know what I'd like for breakfast. I realized that the difference was probably nothing more than a reflection of how Jack had come to terms with his decision and how I could not; but in time, my brother's good spirits became a separate source of anger for me.

On this day, even before he'd made his appearance, I'd vowed to myself that I wasn't going to begin attacking Jack the moment I saw him - not because I didn't *want* to attack him (I did), but because I knew it simply wouldn't work. For a while, I succeeded. We sat together quietly, watching the sunrise, taking in the early morning beauty. The days were becoming increasingly warm, but mornings were still a special time - cool, clear, and crisp. We ate something for breakfast - I cannot remember what. When the sun was high enough, I took a reading with the sextant. Then we sat some more. With the wind out of the south, we were moving along nicely on a broad reach, and there was little in the way of hands-on sailing for either of us to do. It was a quiet time aboard *Sea Legs*, a time unbroken by small talk, a time that would have brought me nothing but absolute delight only a week before. But the longer we sat that day, the more difficult the silence became for me. Here was my brother sitting next to me. In three days, he'd be gone, as they like to say. I forced myself to mouth the word, even silently: *dead*. In three days, he'd be dead, and we weren't even *talking* about it? The more I thought about it, the more ridiculous it struck me. But still I fought the impulse to cry out, so determined was I not to put more pressure on Jack.

I tried to busy myself sailing. I corrected our course, even though we were running just fine; I trimmed sails that really didn't need trimming; I coiled lines as though we were about to be boarded by an inspection committee. I kept myself occupied doing little chores until there were no little chores left to do. And all the while, I seethed inside like a volcano on the brink of erupting. By noon, I'd reached a point where I didn't think I couldn't keep up the charade a moment longer. Yet still I held my tongue.

It was Jack who finally broke the silence. "You seem like you want to talk," he said.

I laughed, a short burst of audible breath that was half bitterness, half relief. "You keep telling me there's nothing to talk about," I reminded him.

"Not exactly," he corrected me, "I've told you I've made up my mind. I've never said I'm unwilling to talk about it."

"That's just great, Jack. You start off by presenting this thing as a done deal, a *fait accompli*. But you're perfectly willing to talk about it. Terrific. Where was I when you first started thinking about it? On the fucking *moon?* Why couldn't you have come to me then, when you say you were trying to decide? Why did you have to wait until you'd made up your mind and dug your heels in?"

Jack took his time answering. "I thought about doing that," he said after a bit. "But the more I thought, the more I realized it had to be my call. It couldn't be anyone else's. Nobody else could possibly have come right out and said yeah, it'd be best if I'd kill myself."

"Doesn't that tell you something?"

Jack smiled. "It tells me that I'm doing something that very few people would do. I pretty much knew that then. I still do."

"How about it tells you you're out of your fucking mind!" I screamed. "What do you think a doctor would tell you?"

"A doctor, like a psychiatrist?"

"No," I said, "a *proctologist*."

"Aha! You think I'm suffering from a case of anocubital confusion?"

"A serious case, I'd say. "As far as I know, it had been our father who'd coined the term *anocubital confusion*. It meant you didn't know your ass from your elbow.

"*Serious* anocubital confusion," Jack intoned. "*Acute* anocubital confusion."

Over the years, a little game had evolved between Jack and me, in which one of us would say something, the other one would top it, and the first would try to top *that*. Jack had said "anocubital confusion," I'd made it "serious." Jack had come back with "acute." It was my turn, but the only word I could think of to top *acute* was *terminal*. So I kept quiet, and the silence that followed was a heavy one. I knew Jack's mind worked exactly the same way as mine did, and it would have brought him to precisely the same word that had occurred to me.

"Yes, a psychiatrist," I said after a while.

"Hmmmm," Jack said "Maybe. 'How do you feel about that?'"

"Careful, you're dating yourself. Nowadays, they don't care how you feel. They just hand you a prescription. Or, if they think you're really serious about killing yourself, they have you committed."

"Committed?" Jack smiled at the thought. "I've never been saner in my life."

"Irrelevant," I said. "The word *sane* is something you find only in crossword puzzles these days. The legal test is whether you're likely to be a danger to yourself or to others. And the way I see it, I'd say you've got a pretty good chance of making the cut."

"Tell you the truth, I'm honestly not all that interested in what some doctor might think," Jack said. "I know what I want to do."

"So does every clown who throws himself off the Golden Gate Bridge," I argued. "Only we know that 90 percent of them are suffering from clinical depression and could easily be treated with medication. How do you know you're not just depressed?"

Jack laughed aloud. But it was a gentle laugh, not unkind, not sarcastic. "Of course I'm depressed," he said. "Death is depressing. Especially when you don't believe there's anything after it. But there's nothing depressing about taking charge of your own life. That feels right."

"Goddamn you! I swear you're *getting off* on killing yourself. You're positively *tripping* on your own death."

Jack seemed to consider this for a moment. "Maybe," he admitted. "Or maybe I'm just feeling okay about being in control of what's going to happen to me, and how it's going to happen. And *when* it's going to happen."

"Maybe you're a goddamned *lunatic!*"

That was the afternoon that Jack hooked his biggest fish - although, at the time, we thought it might be Moby Dick himself at the end of the line.

Jack had become quite the fisherman, sitting at the stern for an hour or so each afternoon and trolling either a lure or a piece of raw fish saved from the previous day's catch. The only tackle we'd brought along was a light rod and a small saltwater spinning reel, so when Jack hooked the fish, the rod bent over almost double and there was an audible *whir* as his line was stripped from his reel.

"Holy shit!" Jack yelled.

"Cut it loose!" I laughed. "It could be a whale, a submarine! It could be the transatlantic *cable,* for Chrissakes!"

"Bring her about! Bring her about!" Jack shouted, and, still laughing, I did my best, easing the sails and heading us into the wind before executing a fancy tacking maneuver that put us on a heading toward whatever monster struggled at the end of Jack's line.

Jack worked his way up to the bow and fought to regain line, while I did my best to steer us in whatever direction the rod seemed to be pointing. It took us a full half hour. We laughed the entire time, speculating on the true identity of our denizen from the deep. Our guesses ran to manta rays, giant squid, undersea volcanos, and Volkswagens. We knew this much: Whatever it was, we had no intention of boating it. We had no gaff or net to land it, and we knew its weight, once we lifted it from the water, would surely snap the light line. Besides, we'd decided early on that it had more than earned its freedom from the fight it was putting up. But we sure wanted to see just what it was that was giving us such a battle.

Eventually, Jack regained enough line so that the creature was brought alongside, almost directly underneath the boat. I turned us into the breeze and let the sails luff, so we drifted to a stop.

"I can see it!" Jack yelled.

I moved forward to join him, to get a look at whatever it was.

"It's a beauty!" I heard him shout.

"What is it?" I asked.

"Looks like a fucking *locomotive!*"

From my angle, all I could see was a telltale dorsal fin cutting through the waves, making a beeline from the west to the spot Jack stood over. Suddenly, there was a violent thrashing in the water, dousing us both, and Jack's rod straightened out. He yanked up on it, and his prize came with it, catapulted over our heads and onto the boat in a single motion. It was a good-sized fish, or, more accurately, a good-sized *half* of a fish. Though it still flipped about on deck, it had been bitten clear through by the shark, which had made off with its tail and much of its body.

"Dolphin," Jack said, and I saw from its vivid coloring that he was right. Not one of the mammal variety - those cousins of the porpoise who'd taken to escorting *Sea Legs* on a fairly regular basis - but the fish, commonly served up to diners under more appetizing names like dorado or mahi-mahi.

The remainder of the fish's struggle was brief. As the life went out of it, its eyes glazed over, and its brilliant rainbow hues faded before us until all that was left was a pale imitation of the living splendor it had been.

Jack scaled the fish and cleaned it, what was left of it, for the shark had done a pretty good job of gutting it. That night, Jack cooked it for dinner and swore it was better even than the flying fish. He called it "mahi," Carib, he explained, for "half a mahi mahi." Me? I couldn't even bring myself to look at it as it lay on my plate. By that time, all it meant to me was death: sudden, wrenching, violent death. An hour before, it had been something majestic, full of color and spirit and will. Now, all of that was gone, forever. All that remained, quite literally, was dead flesh and bones, a terrible image of life reduced to its most basic: an instant spent along the food chain.

That night, as I lay on my bunk, knowing full well that sleep would not come, all I could think of was my only brother being ripped in half and devoured by sharks.

11

Day Three began somewhat later for me than had the several that preceded it. I'd finally fallen asleep sometime before dawn, and when I awoke, it was light outside. My eyes had difficulty adjusting to the brightness. My head ached, and my entire body felt sore. I had all the trappings of a hangover, though I'd had absolutely nothing to drink the night before.

As I climbed up the companionway, I saw Jack, his eyes meeting my own, an index finger raised and pressed against his pursed lips.

I got the message. I hadn't been about to say anything anyway, my head hurt too much for speech. I tiptoed the rest of the way up, to whatever extent a forty-three-year-old man can tiptoe at sea, feeling hungover. I looked again at Jack, whose finger had now evolved into a pointer. I swiveled around to follow its point.

If it did nothing else for me, the sight of a huge bird perched atop our cabin, not five feet from my head, certainly woke me up. I say *huge* not only because it *seemed* so big due to its closeness; I say *huge* because it was, in fact, huge. It was positively *gigantic.*

The bird seemed every bit as startled as I was. But even as I froze, it acted: It turned into the wind, extended its giant wings, flapped them once, and lifted off, leaving me standing there, clutching my heart.

Jack and I watched the bird as it took flight. It was snow white, with a wingspan that must have been over ten feet, and it rode the air currents effortlessly. I was sure I'd frightened it away for good, and that we'd seen the last of it. But as it turned out, I was wrong. The bird made three full circles overhead, each one tighter and lower than the one before it. Then it angled its giant wings forward and glided toward us, all but stopping in midair, before landing perfectly on our transom, within arm's length of Jack, but a safe distance from me.

"What *is* it?" I asked Jack.

"I think it's an emu," he said. "Or maybe an elephant bird."

"Seriously." I wasn't too sure about emus, but I knew elephant birds were extinct.

"Some kind of albatross, I guess. Or a gull with a major thyroid problem?"

"Aren't albatrosses supposed to be bad luck?" Hadn't that been one of the study guide questions following *The Rime of the Ancient Mariner?*

"Only if they're dead, I think."

Right then, the bird made a loud *gawk* noise.

"Careful," Jack said. "You've gone and hurt his feelings."

"His? Looks like a her to me."

"You've just been at sea too long," said Jack.

We settled on *him* after Jack began calling him Gawk, it seemed far too harsh a name for a lady bird. He was clearly partial to Jack and never fully warmed to me (nor I to him, in all fairness). In time, he learned to move about the boat as though it were his, balancing alternately on the transom, the cabin roof, the horseshoe buoy, or the bowsprit - wherever he could be closest to Jack.

I admit to a certain amount of jealousy over this display of favoritism, and more than once I accused Jack of having snuck the bird something to eat before I'd ever set eyes upon him, thereby assuring that the two of them would develop a bond while I'd always be perceived as something of a threat. But the truth was, ever since I could remember, animals and small children had always been drawn to Jack. He was the one who was forever bringing home stray cats, orphaned bunnies, and robins with broken wings. As we grew older, I would sit among the adults at family gatherings, trying to impress them with my social skills, Jack would invariably find himself surrounded by our younger cousins, who would beg him to join them in their games. And as it turned out, I don't think he minded a bit: He seemed more comfortable with animals than with people, and with children than grown-ups. Simple creatures seemed to show no fear of Jack; they somehow found him non-threatening. One of his earliest friends was a badly crippled boy named Cody, who lived down the block. People in the neighborhood referred to him as a "spastic"; we tended to shy away from him, and he from us. But he positively worshiped Jack and was forever following him around and clinging to him. If Jack minded the attention, he didn't once complain about it, and while I'm certain he noticed the boy's deformities along with the rest of us, he never spoke of them; to him, his friend was simply Cody.

Jack did feed Gawk, scraps of this and hits of that, but - despite our worries - Gawk never became dependent upon us for his meals. Whenever the spirit moved him, he'd lift off, climb to some optimal altitude long ago coded into his genetically transmitted survival skills and drilled into his memory by some attentive parent, and execute a perfect dive, breaking the water cleanly at the crest of a wave. More often than not, when he lifted off again, he'd have a fish in his beak, tossing it in midair so that he could swallow it headfirst, while still airborne, before landing back on the boat. So extraordinary were these displays of hunting skills that Jack and I came to believe they were only partly induced by hunger, and primarily motivated by a sheer love of performing. Whatever the truth, we provided him with a most appreciative audience, rating each dive on a scale from one to ten and wildly applauding the best of them.

But Gawk's presence had its own bitter edge for me, and though I never mentioned it aloud, I suspect the thought that occurred to me must have occurred to Jack, as well. Dead or alive, good luck or bad, the arrival of a bird could mean only one thing: We were drawing closer and closer to land. Which meant we were nearing the longitude of the Bermudas, that imaginary vertical band that, when followed due south on our chart, led to a tiny dot of black ink marked "Walker Island."

"Do you believe in God?" I asked Jack that afternoon.

"No," he said. "Not in the usual sense, anyway. You?"

"I sometimes think there's got to be some sort of order to things," I said. "I'm aware that I pray for things sometimes, sort of. You know, like for bad things not to happen, or for people I love to be safe. So I guess I must believe in *something*."

Jack smiled wryly. "Is there by any chance a message in this for me?" he asked.

"Why? Just because every major religion considers suicide a sin that lands you in hell?" I might have been on shaky ground here, taking a bit of license with the facts, but then I figured Jack wasn't much of a theology student.

"How much of a sin could it be," Jack asked, "if it's not a *deadly* sin? If it didn't even make the top seven?"

"Tell that to the Pope, why don't you. Or the head rabbi."

"Anyway, what's a sin?" Jack asked. "Sins are really nothing more than stuff some culture decides is socially unproductive. Ages ago, when everyone lived on farms, there were never enough hands to work the fields. Masturbating became a sin because it didn't produce little baby hoers and weeders. Suicide was a sin because it took away a planter or a goatherd. These days, we've got fewer farms, and high-tech machines to do all the work. And too many mouths to feed. We've got more than enough people."

"Not me," I told him. "You die, there'll never be enough people for me."

"Come on, Joe. You've got your wife, you've got three kids, and you've got all sorts of friends You're *surrounded* by people."

I shook my head slowly. I could feel the tears begin to well up, not too far beneath the surface, but I wasn't ready for them, not yet. "It's not the same," I tried to explain. "Even my wife knows that. She gave up competing with you long ago. Said she realized she'd never have a chance."

"Sorry."

"Don't be sorry," I said. "Not too long ago, she told me that one of the first things that drew her to me was seeing how deeply you and I loved each other. She said she'd never quite seen anything like it between two men."

I looked directly at Jack, and I could see from a tiny quiver barely visible in his lower lip that I'd moved him with this. I said nothing further. I reminded myself I still had two days left to work on the quiver. It was going to work, I told myself. It was going to work.

With the arrival of Gawk, Jack's fishing came to an end. Each time he'd reel in his line, the bird would lift off and make a dive at whatever was on the end of it, whether it was an incoming fish, a slab of bait, or a lure with its gang hooks exposed. After several close calls, Jack was forced to put away his rod and reel for good.

The cancelation of one of the day's regular activities left us with an afternoon of little to do. We were still moving almost due east, making about eight knots on steady winds out of the southwest, and *Sea Legs* was pretty much sailing herself.

I controlled myself for the better part of an hour, trying to enjoy the day, limiting my remarks to small talk. But eventually, I succumbed to the sheer absurdity of avoiding the one topic that consumed my thoughts, and I broke my self-imposed vow of silence on the subject.

"Did you ever think they might come up with a cure?" I asked Jack, pretty much out of the blue.

He gave me a look, as if to say he thought we weren't going to talk about it again so soon. But then he looked away, and he seemed to be considering my question. "Even if they do," he said after a while, "it'd be too late for me."

"Okay," I said. "Suppose instead they come up with a *treatment*. Suppose a month from today, there's a breakthrough, and they discover a drug - or some combination of drugs - that really works, that stops the disease in its tracks. So it'd be like an indefinite remission."

Jack seemed to think about that for a moment, too. "Then I'll have blown it, I guess," he admitted. "But when it comes right down to it, what are the odds of that, really? They've been trying for years, a lot of smart people with all sorts of money. I'm not going to pin my hopes on some magical cure or sudden breakthrough. I don't believe in miracles. Not that sort, anyway."

"Oh? And what sort of miracles *do* you believe in?"

"The miracle of having lived," he said. "Of having been lucky enough to have had this time with you. Of having come through that storm in one piece. Of knowing we did it."

I said nothing.

"Anyway," Jack said, smiling, "I'll never know. But then again, I'll also never know if my decision is going to deprive me of seeing world peace in our lifetime, or UFOs landing, or the Sox winning the World Series. I could wait, hoping for all of those things to happen in the meantime. Hey, I can think of a thousand reasons to delay. The problem is, after a while, delaying becomes a decision all its own. It has its possibilities, sure, but it also has its price. I guess all I'm saying is, I'm not willing to pay the price required to keep those possibilities open. They're simply too remote. So the way I see it, now becomes the right time."

"If Jack refused to waver in his decision, at least I began to notice that his tone was becoming a little less strident. Expressions like "the way I see it" and "it seems to me" had begun to find their way into his vocabulary. And each time I'd hear him use such a phrase, I'd take heart. Was my desperation so great that I was simply grasping at straws, or was I, in fact, picking up some signal that, as we drew nearer and nearer to our destination, Jack's resolve was weakening just a bit, his shell of stubbornness beginning to show the first signs of cracking?

I dared to hope.

12

A new sight greeted us the following morning. Far to the southwest, a pair of ships were headed more or less our way, on a bearing that would intersect ours as they continued east-northeast. It had been weeks since we'd seen another vessel; now, all of a sudden, we'd spotted two.

Jack peered at them through high-powered binoculars before announcing, "Cruise ships."

My initial wave of excitement gave way to a sobering thought. They could be headed only to Bermuda, I knew, out of Charleston or Savannah or some other port farther down the coast. The fact that they were passing us here meant they were less than a day from their destination, and that we, even sailing at a fraction of their speed, couldn't be too far from ours.

I took a shot of the sun with my sextant and found our coordinates from the conversion tables. For some reason, I still took comfort in the ritual of dead reckoning. It was like going back to a place I'd visited so often as a child that I knew the way by heart, or coming to the familiar refrain of a favorite song. I marked our position on the chart, did some rough calculations, and reassured myself that we still had a full day's sailing ahead of us.

Although, at first, the ships appeared to be close to each other, as they approached, we could see that they were actually far apart, perhaps as much as several miles. One would cross well behind our wake, it appeared, but the second would pass quite near us.

I was suddenly seized by the possibilities of the situation. Even if they hadn't spotted us yet on their radar, there'd come a time when the crew of the second boat would have to see us. Should I try signaling them? We carried a full array of emergency flares on board, all I'd have to do would be to send up a distress signal, and they'd be forced to lower a boat to assist us.

I created scenarios in which I persuaded the rescue party that Jack was suicidal, deranged, or sick. In my mind, I talked them into taking us both aboard, even lifting tiny *Sea Legs* onto their deck. Surely a ship that size would have a hoist of some sort. And it would have a *lockup*. I'd convince them my brother was a murderer, a fugitive from justice who needed to be put in restraints.

Nearer and nearer the second ship drew as it bore down on us, until its hugeness rose above us and we could make out the shapes of passengers on deck. Then, just as I began to fear that she might swamp us with her giant wake, she gave us two long blasts of her horn and veered off to the north, so that she'd pass us on her starboard side, well off our stern. Jack acknowledged her signal with two blasts from our own air horn, though by that time, the roar of her engines was so loud that I'm sure our response was inaudible.

As she passed directly behind us, early-morning risers crowded to her starboard rail to call to us and wave. We couldn't make out what it was they were shouting, but we cheerfully returned their waves. We were even able to read the name painted in pink letters on her white hull: *Endless Summer.*

At this point Gawk, who had apparently spent the night with us, suddenly lifted off and made a beeline for the ship. To the delight of her passengers, he made three perfect circles over their heads and dipped low in an aborted dive before returning to *Sea Legs* and resuming his perch on our transom.

It was a good twenty minutes later, as I watched the ship and its companion vessel recede into the distance, that I realized I'd completely forgotten about my plan to send up a distress signal.

But if I failed to follow through on my fantasy of enlisting the crew of the *Endless Summer* to restrain Jack, I showed him little mercy the rest of that morning. I'd just commented on Gawk's impressive display of loyalty to us, pointing out that the bird would surely have found better roosting - not to mention bigger hand-outs - aboard the cruise ship.

"Maybe he picked us out for some reason," Jack suggested.

"Oh? And what might that be?"

"Who knows? Maybe he's been sent to me as some sort of an escort."

I'd been busy with some chore at the moment. Now I wheeled around to face my brother. "What did you say?"

"You heard me."

"I was hoping I got it wrong," I said.

"Sorry." Jack shrugged.

"Listen to yourself!" I shouted. "You're really full of yourself, aren't you? Now the goddamned *bird* has been sent here to escort you? Give me a break, man! Your problem is that you're positively overdosing on self-pity!"

"I've actually thought about that," Jack said, "and you may be right. Hey, I've spent a lot of time trying to figure out what ulterior motives I may have going on here. You know, like pure cowardice? Or maybe it's a martyrdom thing - my desperate striving for adoration, trying to carve out my niche as a family legend. I've even asked myself if it might not be my way of winning some ultimate competition with you, some bottom-of-the-ninth getting even."

"And?"

"And," he said, "I've decided it's just not all that complicated." Here he locked the wheel in place so that he could turn to face me without distraction. "Listen," he said, "I know how hard you've been trying to get me to see things through your eyes, I really do. But I need you to spend a little time trying to see them through *my* eyes. I've thought about this more than I've ever thought about anything in my life, trust me. And I end up honestly believing I'm doing this for no reason other than the one I've given you. I've lived a wonderful life, Joe, I've had a fabulous trip, especially this last leg of it with you. I wouldn't have given that up for anything. But I know what's ahead, and I don't want any part of it. That's it. That's all there is to it."

"You make it sound like it's all so fucking simple," I said.

"It is, really."

"Then why do I feel like my guts are being ripped out of my body?"

"I'm sorry for that," Jack said softly.

"No, you're not," I told him. "You love it. You wouldn't have it any other way."

I kept up a steady barrage all that day. I was sarcastic; I was confrontational; I was accusatory. I gave up all pretense of backing off and giving Jack room to breathe.

"You want to know something, Jack?" I asked, without pausing to hear if he wanted to or not. "For the rest of my life, to the day I die, I'll be left with the knowledge that - as far as you were concerned - I wasn't worth living for. How do you think that's going to make me feel?"

"Really terrible," Jack said, "if that's what you're going to reduce it all to. But we both know it's not about that."

"Oh? Maybe *you* know," I said. "Me, I have no *idea* what it's about. Not really."

"Then you haven't been listening to me."

"Fuck *you*" I shouted. "I've been listening to you till I want to throw up!"

"Hey," Jack said, "save your strength. You're going to be needing it for the trip back."

For some reason, the thought of sailing back alone didn't terrify me as much as it should have. Perhaps the storm had knocked all the terror out of me, I don't know. Whatever the reason, I never did get around to playing that particular card, accusing Jack of leaving me in actual physical danger. But I sure played every other card in the deck.

"Maybe I won't go back," I told him. "Maybe I'll just throw myself in right after you, see how you deal with it."

"You won't do that," Jack said calmly.

"And why not?"

"Because, when it comes right down to it, you and I are different. I'm a quitter, we now see. All this time, I've only been here for the good times. Now that the heat's about to get turned up, I'm getting out of the kitchen. You, you're a survivor, Joe. You're on board for the long haul."

"I'll never forgive you, you bastard," I swore at him at one point.

"Yes you will," Jack said. "Anyway, last I checked, forgiveness was somebody else's department."

"Don't get pious with me, you hypocrite!" I shouted. "You who don't believe in anything!"

"That's not fair," he said. "I believe in all sorts of things."

"Like what?"

"Like love," he said. "Like living."

"Then *live!*" I screamed. "Live for *me,* for *my* sake, if for nothing else." By the time I'd finished spitting out the words, I'd gone from railing at him to begging him. I collapsed into a sitting position, holding my head in my hands. A moment later, I felt Jack's hand on my back. Again I felt tears welling up, trying to surface, but I fought them off. I was still far too angry to give Jack the satisfaction of seeing me break down. And I was still determined to win this war of wills. I *had* to, I told myself: Nothing less than my brother's life hung in the balance, and - or so it felt at the time at least - so did mine.

The day wore on without Jack showing any signs of relenting. He seemed relaxed and at peace with his decision, and perfectly content to continue sailing on, quite literally, as though everything were just fine. As for me, with every passing hour, I grew more and more agitated. I couldn't eat, I couldn't sleep, and I finally reached a point where I refused to engage my brother in the kind of small talk he seemed to expect of me. By evening, I was a wreck, totally exhausted and physically ill, too strung out to lie down, too upset to eat or drink.

"Keep it up," Jack said at one point, trying to coax me to sip some iced tea he'd made, "and we'll both end up dead."

"Good" was all I said, and I meant it; I swear I did.

"I guess you've finally figured out a way to make me feel guilty."

"Good," I repeated. "You've got plenty to feel guilty about."

When you're on the ocean, there's almost always a breeze, and you can easily be fooled into thinking it's pleasantly cool on even the hottest of days. As a result, you've got to be constantly replenishing body fluids, or you'll grow dehydrated before you know it. By that nightfall, I'd developed a fever and was experiencing intermittent bouts of chills and sweats. I remember Jack's face appearing over mine at one point, threatening to pour a bottle of water down my throat if I wouldn't drink it on my own. I gave in finally, not out of thirst or any desire to live, but because, by that time, I was simply too weak to resist him.

I spent the night drifting in and out of delirium. If Jack woke me once, he must have woken me twenty times, on each occasion lifting my head and forcing me to drink before he'd lower me gently and allow me to drift off again. I dreamt wild, violent, vividly colored nightmares - of my brother being carried aloft in the talons of some giant bird of prey while I screamed in protest from the spiraling vortex of a powerful whirlpool that sucked me ever deeper and deeper under the water.

13

I awoke the next morning with my clothes and covers drenched from my own sweat. But my fever had broken, and my delirium was gone. Once again, as he had during the night of the storm, my brother had come to my rescue. Once again, his strength had saved me from my weakness,

Obediently, I drank juice and even ate some breakfast that was put before me, the first real food I'd taken in several days. I knew full well that Jack was nursing me back to health so that I'd be strong enough to turn the boat around when the time came and head for home, but I complied anyway. The thought occurred to me that by continuing my hunger strike, by again refusing to drink, I might force him to abandon - or at least postpone - his plan. But I was beyond protesting by then; I was beaten.

I spent the day staring out over the ocean, wondering how something I'd once regarded as incredibly majestic and soothing was soon to be turned into an agent of destruction - to my only brother's watery grave.

Once or twice I succumbed to my old self, momentarily convinced I could still talk Jack out of his plan. "How about let's keep right on sailing?" I begged at one point. "We can make it clear to Africa, I bet."

"Stop being the lawyer," Jack told me gently. "Stop trying to negotiate a settlement. It's over. Let me go."

And, God help me, I obeyed him. I did as I was told: I stopped. And in my stopping, by the very act of my wordless acquiescence, I acknowledged that it was over; I agreed to let him go. I gave my younger brother my blessing, my permission for him to take leave of this life.

And Jack saw all this, I know, and somehow understood it, because he held my eyes with his and spoke but two words to me, almost in a whisper.

"Thank you" is what he said.

Then, finally, did my tears come: great, huge body-racking sobs that threatened to suck all the air from my lungs and dry up all the water from my blood. I doubled over in agony, I writhed on the cockpit floor; I broke capillaries in my eyelids and tore blood vessels in my throat. I have no idea how long I cried, it seemed like hours. I cried until I had no more tears, and still I cried. Jack held me, he let me go, he held me again. He cried with me, he let me cry alone. But he knew enough to say not a word; there were no words to say.

Eventually, I reached the point where I was cried out, where I'd simply arrived at a place *beyond* crying. And then we sat, my brother and I, in each other's arms, still saying nothing, and we watched the sun slide down the western sky behind us.

And that evening, when by the last of my sextant readings we both knew full well that we'd finally come to that spot in the ocean where Walker Island was supposed to have been, if only there had been a Walker Island, Jack kissed my mouth with his and placed his hand lightly on the side of my face. After a moment, he let his hand travel slowly, softly, ever so softly down my cheek, almost as though he was trying to commit to memory the very shape and texture of my face. Then he rose from my side, stepped to the starboard rail, and slipped silently into the water.

14

If you were to ask me how it was that I managed to turn *Sea Legs* toward home, I could not tell you. After I watched Jack slip into the water, I must have taken the wheel, brought her about, and set a course to the west, as though in some futile attempt to chase down the last of the fading twilight. But the truth is, I have no recollection whatsoever of doing any of those things.

First light found my hands glued to the wheel. For all I know, they'd been there all night. I know I could just as easily have left things to the self-steering system, but I imagine I felt the need of something to do, some activity to keep me going through the night.

And in that same first light, I came to notice that Gawk was nowhere on board. I searched the sky for him all that day, hoping to spot him circling effortlessly overhead or diving toward the rise of a cresting wave. But I must have known he was gone for good. Had he simply taken off on some sudden whim? Had he been a purposeful hitchhiker, determined to find another vessel as he made his way ever east to the Old World? Or had some internal compass told him that we'd finally reached the longitude of the Bermudas, where land lay, over the curve of the horizon, some 200 miles to the north? Then I remembered Jack's comment that perhaps the bird had been sent as some sort of an escort for him. The rational part of me rejected the notion outright, just as I had when Jack had first suggested it. Still, I couldn't ignore the fact that in a single night, both of them had been taken from me. I just didn't know whether I should be consoled by the coincidence or feel doubly devastated.

I know I resumed the business of dead reckoning: I have the log to tell me that. At first, I wrote little more than a few lines a day. I find, for example, the following complete entry, a day or two into my return trip:

> Sailed due west, 180 mag., all day and all night. Made 157 naut. miles.

Several days later, I'd become only slightly more expansive:

> Continued on heading 175 mag. Made 163 naut. miles. Spotted giant whale 100 yds off bow. Think it was a blue.

I know I ate and drank and slept and steered, but I know these things only because I survived, not because I have any real recollection of them. I remember hitting some weather though it was nothing like the storm Jack and I had encountered on the way out. I do recall seeing a giant waterspout at one point, a seagoing version of a twister. Spouts are not all that uncommon on the ocean, where there's nothing in the way of topography to slow down winds or break up turbulence, but neither Jack nor I had ever seen one before, and this was a beauty. For a moment, it looked to be headed directly at me, but I felt no particular sense of panic: I suppose a good portion of me would have welcomed death at that point. Instead, my only reaction was how beautiful it was, how absolutely spectacular, and how terribly painful it was that Jack wasn't there to share it with me.

If I ate and drank and slept enough to survive, I barely did so. By the time I reached land, I'd lost almost thirty pounds, though I don't know how much of that had happened before I'd turned around. I was badly burned, not having remembered to guard against the summer sun. My teeth were rotting from eating poorly and forgetting to brush them. My clothes were dirty and, I'm told, foul-smelling.

About a week offshore, the wind shifted until it came out of the west and into my face. I tried tacking for a while, heading first northwest, then southwest, but it proved dreadfully slow. I gave it up, and instead set a course to the southwest, figuring I'd put in wherever it took me.

Two days off, I began seeing other boats, and many of them approached to hail me, evidently thinking I was some kind of hero who'd sailed clear across the Atlantic. But I waved them off, determined to bring *Sea Legs* in myself, under sail. Jack would have been proud of me, I figured.

I made landfall down the coast of South Carolina, not too far from Port Royal Sound, at a little spit of land named, ironically enough, Journey's End. I paid in cash for a week's stay at a boatyard, packed up a duffel bag, and hitched a ride into Savannah, where I holed up in a third-rate motel.

All this time, I'd had no radio contact with family or friends. I knew I had to check in with my wife, who, I assumed, by this time must have been frantic with worry. But I also knew I couldn't call without telling her of Jack's death, and for some reason I dreaded that more than anything. It was almost as though it was my secret, my private shame; but once I reported it, it would be out there for the whole world to know, and, in knowing, to judge me and blame me.

I bought a quart bottle of dark rum; it seemed an appropriate-enough selection. I drank half of it, sitting on the bed in my room. But I got sick before I got drunk, and when I finally reached for the phone to dial home sometime after midnight, my hand still trembled visibly.

My wife answered on the first ring, with alarm in her voice. I managed to say hello and tell her I was safe and on dry land. We talked for a moment, each of us saying how good it was to hear the other's voice. Then there was a pause, during which I waited for the inevitable.

"How's Jack?" she asked.

And the tears came flooding back. In torrents they came, in oceans. I could not speak; I could not utter a single word. Finally, I simply gave up trying. I placed the receiver back in the cradle of the phone.

Somehow my wife managed to find out where I was, and she flew down to meet me. Over my protestations, she had me driven to a hospital, where I was admitted, diagnosed with exposure, dehydration, malnutrition, and assorted other ailments. They kept me three days, during which time my wife never left my side, feeding me, bathing me, and sleeping each night in a cot beside my bed. The violent nightmares returned, and I'm told I did my share of ranting and raving.

When they discharged me, we flew back north, leaving *Sea Legs* behind in the boatyard. I spent another month recuperating at home. There were visits from my children, and from Jack's daughters and ex-wife. His girls seemed to accept the story of his being washed overboard during the height of the storm; his ex-wife was a different story. She came one day when I was sitting downstairs in the sunroom. I still wasn't ready to venture outside. She sat opposite me, the sunlight falling across her in horizontal lines created by the window blinds. For a long time, she just looked at me, and I tried my best to look at her. Then she asked me a single question, the only thing she said to me the whole time she was there that day.

"Was he afraid, at the very end?" is what she asked.

I forced myself to look her in the eye. "No," I said. "He wasn't afraid. He was never afraid."

The people from the boatyard down in Journey's End called, asking if someone would be picking up *Sea Legs*. For a while, my wife tried to talk me into flying down and bringing her up the Intracoastal, or hiring someone to do it, or even renting a trailer to haul her north. But as much as I'd once loved the boat, I no longer wanted anything to do with her; I knew my sailing days were over. We arranged with a broker in Savannah to sell her and ship us what remained of our belongings.

I have not been to sea since. To this day, I am unable to step aboard a commuter ferry. I cannot take a rowboat out on a pond, or paddle a canoe across a lake. Sailing was once one of the great loves of my life. It's not a matter of missing it now, or not missing it; it's simply something I no longer do, and never will again.

I know full well that everybody who lives also dies. I lost my grandparents growing up. Both my parents died when they were still in their sixties. And when my children first learned to drive, I became obsessed with their mortality, and my heart stopped each time the phone rang in the middle of the night, when one of them was out. But in my wildest dreams, it never occurred to me that my own kid brother would die before I would. Nothing prepared me for that. *Nothing.*

A year or two ago, I was leafing through a magazine, a *National Geographic,* it may have been, and I came across a photo of a giant seabird. I found myself staring at it, without quite understanding why. Then it hit me: I was looking at Gawk. I read the caption.

> The Wandering Albatross *(Diomedea exulans)* The largest member of the albatross family, the wandering albatross reaches a length of four feet and a wingspan of twelve feet. It mates for life and, if separated, is said to wander over the oceans forever, in search of its lost mate.

Not a day of my life goes by that I don't think of Jack. I still dream of him often, though the dreams are no longer violent. Perhaps that's progress of some sort. But to this day, I'll be walking down the street, and I'll spot some wiry young man with touches of gray in his hair, and my heart will stop. Then he'll turn my way and reveal to me that he's not my brother after all. My brother is dead, I have to remind myself. He killed himself.

Was he right to do what he did, when he did it? To this day, I don't know the answer to that, any more than I did fifteen years ago. I know it was wrong for me, horribly, excruciatingly wrong. But I also know that in the fifteen years since Jack's death, nobody has come up with a cure for the disease that surely would have killed him by this time. No UFOs have landed that I know of. And the Sox haven't even come close to winning a World Series.

I've spent a lot of hours and a lot of dollars listening to some very educated people telling me that it's time for me to stop thinking I let Jack down and to begin to realize that it was the other way around. I understand I'm supposed to be angry at Jack for that. But how can I be angry at him? I love him too much. I miss him too much, still.

My own life goes on. I practice law; I write my books. I have a wonderful wife and three terrific children. I'm even a grandfather these days. By all accounts, I should be the happiest man alive. And the truth is that I am, in many ways. Until the end of the day, that is, when I close my eyes. Then do I feel his mouth on mine, his hand moving ever so softly down the side of my face. And once again my only brother rises from beside me and slips silently into the sea.

Made in the USA
Lexington, KY
21 July 2019